The
Survival
of
Sarah Landing

MARGARET MEACHAM

The Survival of Sarah Landing

FIRST SUNBURY PRESS EDITION
Printed in the United States of America
November 2012

Trade Paperback ISBN: 978-1-62006-158-9
Mobipocket format (Kindle) ISBN: 978-1- 62006-159-6
ePub format (Nook) ISBN: 978-1-62006-160-2

Published by:
Sunbury Press
Mechanicsburg, PA
www.sunburypress.com

Mechanicsburg, Pennsylvania   USA

To my family,
John,
Pete and Hanako,
Jen and John
And K-Bird
With so much love and thanks for
putting up with me

To Sal,
For listening, laughing
and always understanding

And to Charles,
A friend indeed

Acknowledgments

I'm so grateful to early readers Jenny Bailey, Rena Diana, Lizz Smith, Suzanne Supplee, Missy Unkovic and Rachel Unkovic for their advice, encouragement and support.

Many thanks to Mike and Margot McConnel for inviting me home to the Eastern Shore, and putting me up so often while I was working on this book.

I'm indebted to my favorite mystery writers whose works I have loved and studied over the years: Kate Atkinson, Agatha Christie, Tana French, Elizabeth George, Laura Lippman, Louise Penny, and Dorothy Sayers, to name just a few.

With dear thanks to the members of the Molly Brown Book Club for 20 years of insightful discussions, delicious dinners, and treasured friendships.

And to publishers Lawrence and Tammi Knorr, editor Allyson Gard, and the other folks at Sunbury for their insights, support and professional expertise.

And as always, to my dear family and friends for their love and support, and from whom many of the funnier parts of this book were "borrowed."

It is cold out on the river on this late September night. And dark. There is no moon, and though the stars are bright, they don't provide much light. The tide is turning, and a slight breeze carries a muddy, low tide smell.

From the shore the cicadas sing their last songs of summer, an owl hoots, and in the distance there is the sound of a boat's engine running toward the Bay. The boat is too far away to hear the quiet creak of the oars, the soft lap of the water as the little pram cuts through it.

When the pram is far off shore, out in the middle of the river, the wind picks up, and it is time. The oars are stowed. A figure rises. There is a splash, a glow of phosphorescence, and then the gruesome bundle is gone, sinking slowly, slowly to her watery grave.

Once again, the oars creak, the water laps. The figure, hunched and alone considers following her into the water, but rows on. It didn't have to be this way. If only she had listened. For so many years she had listened, and she had done as she was told. If only she hadn't stopped listening.

Chapter One

I knew the manuscript was good the minute I looked at it. Better than good. It was great. And it was inspiring. Something about it flipped a switch in my brain, a switch that had been off for almost three years, and I was able to work again. Maybe that's one reason why it became so important to me to find out what had happened.

In the weeks before it had come, I had been struggling desperately to make some progress on my work. For one thing, we were running out of money. Granted, I had decided to adopt a blithe, devil-may-care attitude about the situation. The roof was leaking? Ha ha, what was a little water? The mortgage company was threatening to foreclose- oh well, living in the Bronco could be fun. So cozy! So compact!

But it was more than that. The money situation was bad, but it wasn't as bad as not being able to work. I wanted to work. I needed to work. I was desperate to work.

In my twelve step program for grieving spouses, we were advised to trust that our higher power will take care of things. I had been trying; trying to believe that things would fall into place, that my once wonderfully amenable muse would come back from her vacation and help me get my new picture book underway. But they hadn't. And she hadn't. Hello? Higher power? Could you just ring up the muse and tell her vacation's over? That's all. A simple phone call. Is that too much to ask?

The day the manuscript came was cool and clear. It was still early September, but there was a definite hint of fall in the air. I was in my office, struggling as usual, staring out the window, and watching the water fairies dancing on the creek- Tom's grandmother's term for the shimmering rays of sunlight reflected on the water. Peach Blossom Creek was in full glory that morning, and the possibility that we might have to move was a hurricane-sized cloud on my horizon.

My meeting with Donald Brace, our mortgage banker, was still three weeks away, but I was already dreading it. Brace was about as empathetic as a cantaloupe, but I hoped that even he would hesitate to foreclose on a widow with three children. Especially if I cried. And I would cry. I wouldn't even have to fake it.

The day passed with nothing but a Mt. Everest sized pile of crumpled paper to show for it, and it was a relief when I heard Geordie coming up the walk and I knew that, at least until another night had passed, I could stop this torturous, paper- wasting process.

Geordie had picked up the mail from our box at the end of the drive as he often did. As soon as he and Paddington, our bear sized Chesapeake Bay Retriever, had finished their love fest, he handed me the usual bundle of bills and ⅟ held out a padded manila mailer. "What's this, Mom?" he asked, studying the package suspiciously.

"I don't know, honey. Let's see." I took the package from him and looked it over. Apparently someone had hand delivered it because there was no address, only my name, Sarah Landing, written in large, square, capital letters.

"I hope it's not a mail bomb," Geordie said. Geordie was eight going on sixty-five, with a serious penchant for worrying. He could out worry my seventy-six year old uncle any day of the week. His favorite bedtime story book was the *Worst Case Scenario Survival Handbook*. He could tell you what to do in case of alligator attack, immersion in quicksand, or volcanic eruption. Unfortunately he had no solutions for writer's block or failing bank accounts. Actually, none of the children had any idea how serious our financial situation was. I figured they had enough to

2

worry about without that, and I'd tried to keep it from them.

I opened the flap of the mailer and found a manuscript pressed between two pieces of cardboard and secured with rubber bands. A note scribbled on one of the pieces of cardboard said "Dear Ms. Landing, I will be taking your course at the Arts Center this fall and I was hoping you might have a chance to look this over before class. Many thanks." It was signed Louisa Myner.

"Just a manuscript from one of my students," I told Geordie, putting it back in the mailer. I'll deal with it later."

I looked over the rest of the mail and heard the thuds and thumps that signal Justin's return. Paddington raced to the door, greeting him enthusiastically. Justin dropped his back pack and said, "Hey, girl. Hey, Paddy. Yeah, I missed you too."

He came into the kitchen and put his fist out to Geordie who met it with his own. "Hey, bro. Hi, Mom," he said, tripping over a chair and knocking over my tea mug.

"Careful, Jus," I said.

He grunted and made his way to refrigerator. Justin, having grown six inches in the last three months, was over six feet tall, and often had trouble managing his limbs. He seemed to forget that he could actually control his arms, and they tended to swing dangerously. I was always nervous when he was in a small place. Also, recently his vocabulary had dwindled alarmingly to a caveman-like system of grunts and groans. He was quite verbal as a young child, but now, at fourteen, it seemed he could hardly cobble together two or three words. It was as if, with his new growth, his brain was doing all it could to keep his limbs and vital organs relatively under control. Mouth, tongue and vocal chords were on their own, temporarily. At least, I hoped it was temporary. He opened the fridge and began his daily ritual of systematically consuming its entire contents.

"What happened to your hair?" Geordie asked.

"You like it?"

I turned around to look at him. He had taken off his baseball cap, and I saw that his normally brown hair was a blindingly bright shade of pumpkin. What *had* happened, I

3

wondered. Could this have been caused by some freak accident of nature? That seemed a more likely explanation than anyone, even Justin, actually choosing this color.

"It's kind of, um, bright," Geordie said, tactfully I thought.

"Bix got this hair dye. You should see his if you think mine is bright."

"Cool," Geordie said.

"Is it, uh, permanent?" I asked.

Justin shrugged. "Not sure. Prob'ly,"

"Well, it'll grow out eventually, I suppose," I said.

Another shrug and a grunt, and he resumed his place half way into the fridge.

Enter Grace, who screamed when she saw Justin. "God! What happened to him?"

"Apparently he and Bix had a run in with a bottle of hair color," I explained.

"You're going to...let him keep it like that?"

"It'll grow out."

She dropped her backpack and headed upstairs. "I've got to go to Julie's. She needs to borrow my Spanish book."

In a few minutes she came back, wearing a new pair of very pointed, very high heeled shoes.

"Goodness. Where did those come from?" I asked.

"I got them at Shoe Emporium yesterday when Cary and I went shopping. I used my own money," she added quickly, fending off any complaints I might have. Grace worked Saturday and Sunday mornings at the Good Penny Bakery in town. "Mom, can I use the car just to go over to Julie's? I'll be right back."

Grace had her learner's permit and was unable to comprehend the fact that a learner's permit is not a driver's license.

"Sweetie, you know the answer to that," I said.

"Mom, it's a quarter mile away."

"Then it shouldn't be a problem for you to walk or ride a bike. Hurry though. Dinner's in an hour."

"I'll ride my bike," she said.

"Fine. You might want to change your shoes though." Call me crazy, but four inch stilettos don't strike me as the ideal footwear for biking.

"These are the only shoes I have, Mom."

Oh? What would one call the forty shoe- shaped objects in her closet? "What about your running shoes?" I asked.

"Mom! God! With these pants? You're joking, right?"

Later that night, Geordie and I were curled up on his bed reading *Prince Caspian*, book three of C.S. Lewis's *Narnia* series. When I finished the chapter and put the book aside, Geordie said, "You know there's a thing called survival camp, Mom. I think I should go."

"Oh, honey, you don't need survival camp. You already know everything about survival."

"It sounds cool though. Benjy was telling me about it. They give you one match and drop you in the wilderness, and you have to survive all by yourself for three days."

"That's Outward Bound, I think. But it's for older kids. Maybe when you're older you can go."

Was this survival stuff weird enough to constitute a problem, I wondered, or was it just his way of coping? Geordie had only been five years old when his dad, my husband Tom, had been killed. Tom had been coming home from a business meeting in Baltimore when the steering cable in a tractor trailer had snapped, causing the truck to swing into the oncoming lane where Tom's car hit it head on. Tom had died instantly, at least, I hope and pray he had, because he was dead ten minutes later when the police got to the scene. I try to believe that he never knew what hit him, and that his last thoughts were of something terribly ordinary, like what we'd be having for dinner, and how Grace's soccer tryouts had gone.

"Can Benjy come for a sleepover on Friday?" Geordie asked.

"Sure, honey. Or you could go there," I said hopefully, because Benjy had come here the last ten or so times the boys had gotten together.

"No. We like my house better."

"That's fine, then. I'll call his mom tomorrow."

"Good. 'Night, Mom,"

"'Night, Sweetie." I kissed him good night and went downstairs to finish cleaning up.

As I was on my way up to bed, I remembered the

package. I took it upstairs with me, opened it again, removed the cardboard, and saw for the first time the manuscript that would so profoundly alter several lives, my own among them.

I looked at the cover illustration. Water color over delicate pen and ink drawings. It was lovely and exceedingly well done. *Jesse's Secret* by Louisa Myner. I turned to the first page and began to read. By the fifth page, I felt something stirring in the pit of my stomach. It was good. It was really, really good. Louise Myner, who ever she was, was talented.

It was the story of a boy, Jesse, who befriends a homeless man named Duncan. Jesse begins leaving little gifts of food and small change and other things he thinks will help Duncan. When the homeless man finds out who the gifts are coming from he wants to give Jesse something in return. He makes a small wood carving, something he hasn't been able to do in years, though he was once a talented carver.

I liked the story. I was impressed with the spare, powerful language, and the way the writer managed to avoid sentimentality. And the illustrations were consistently beautiful. It was rare to find such talent, especially in a student. So often the work I saw from my students was hackneyed and trite, amateurish at best, but this was an accomplished work of art, and I thought it actually had a chance, a good chance, of finding a publisher.

One of things I tried to hide from my students was that, even if they had talent, determination and persistence, their chances of getting a children's book published in today's market were about as good as their chances of finding a chest full of pirate's treasure buried under their rosebushes, possibly slightly worse. It could happen, but you didn't want to quit your day job on the chance.

But a manuscript like this...maybe I was overreacting, but this was something special.

I was sitting in bed reading *Jesse's Secret* over again when Grace came in to say goodnight.

"Home work all done?" I asked her

6

"Yup. Except I have to study a bit more for the history test tomorrow. I have second period free." She lay down beside me on the bed, and I smoothed the hair off her forehead, loving the feel of her soft, warm skin. Grace was so lovely. I sometimes found it hard to believe that Tom and I actually created this amazing creature. "What's this, Mom?" she asked picking up the manuscript.

"It's a picture book manuscript. From a student who will be in my new class."

She looked at the cover and began to read, studying the art work closely. "Wow," she said when she had read about five pages. "This is good, isn't it, Mom?"

"It is."

"Louisa Myner," she read. "Do you know her?"

"No. But I'm anxious to meet her."

"How's your new book coming, Mom?'

"It's coming," I said. A lie, but I didn't want to worry her. The truth was, since Tom's death three years ago, I really hadn't done anything. My last two books, A Dog's Life and A Cat's Life had both sold well, and my publisher was hoping for more of the same, but they seemed weightless and silly to me now. A Cat's Life was almost completed when he died, and I had managed to finish it up and get it to my publisher a year later. It had come out 18 months ago and fortunately had sold very well. It was a good thing, because if it wasn't for those royalties and the advance I had gotten on the strength of its success, we would be in even worse financial shape then we were.

"So, what is it about?" she asked.

Good question. "Well, I'm, umm, not really ready to talk about it yet."

"Oh, I see. The mysterious artist, huh?"

"Something like that," I said.

"Okay, Mom. Whatever." She yawned. "I gotta get to bed." She kissed me and then jumped off the bed, attempted, somewhat clumsily, a ballerina style leap across the room, twirled once, and waved over her shoulder as she went out the door. I smiled. That was Grace.

7

Chapter Two

The following morning I put Louisa Myner's manuscript in a drawer in the desk in my office. I would give it a week, look it over again, and if I still felt the same way, I would call Louisa and arrange to meet her before our first class session, still three weeks away.

I'm not sure why, but there was something inspiring about Louisa's manuscript and about the prospect of being able to help her get published. It made me want to get right to work on my own book. I picked up my charcoal pencil and began to draw.

I drew a creature. I wasn't sure what kind of creature it was; it was just a creature. I gave him a wand, and a wizard's cloak, though he was a funny fat little creature, not at all wizard-like. The creature was just playing at being a wizard. Pretending he knew what he was doing. Pretending he was in control.

I worked on him most of the day that day, and by evening the funny, furry creature became more defined. He kept his wizard's cloak and his wand, and his features became familiar. I liked him, but I didn't want to think too much about him for fear he would go away and never come back. I kept drawing him though, over and over in different poses, sometimes sitting on the floor of his room, his short legs out in front of him and a look of concentration on his face, sometimes out in his back yard, lying on his back in the grass, looking up at the sky through a ceiling of new spring leaves. Yes. I liked him, and I was getting to know him.

I was just about ready to stop for the day when the call came from Pinnacle. I had been avoiding Julia's calls for months, but this time I picked up without looking at the caller ID.

"May I speak with Sarah Landing, please?" It was a male voice.

"This is Sarah."

"Yes. Hello. My name is Daniel Hollister. I'm from Pinnacle Books?"

"Oh, Well, hi," I said, guardedly. Maybe he was from bookkeeping, threatening to take back the advance if I didn't come up with a manuscript soon.

"Yes, I don't know if you've spoken with Julia?" He sounded hesitant, almost embarrassed. Surely Julia herself would call if they were canceling my contract? Or she would have called Katharine Briggs, my agent, and had her do the dirty work.

"No, No I've been, um, I haven't. Well, not for several weeks at least," I told him.

"You probably haven't heard then that she's leaving Pinnacle?"

"Julia's leaving?"

"She is. Well, actually, she's already left. I'm surprised she hasn't been in touch with you herself."

"Well, as a matter of fact, she may have tried. My answering machine has been on the fritz. People can leave messages, but I can't retrieve them. So frustrating." This was a lie I had told so often lately I was beginning to believe it.

"Ah yes. The miracle of voicemail." There was a slight pause and then he went on. "The reason I'm calling, actually, is to introduce myself. I'll be your new editor, and I must tell you, I love your work. I'm really looking forward to working with you."

"I see. Well, that's great. Thank you."

"I'm sure this must come as somewhat of a shock to you, but I promise the transition will be easy. "

9

"Uh huh," I was thinking that it would be very easy, since, for the last year and a half, there had been nothing to edit, no work to discuss.

"I was wondering, actually, if I might come by and see you," he said.

"Come by here?" I said, stupidly.

"Yes. I'll be in DC the end of this month, and I thought it would be nice to meet you in person."

"I see. Well, yes, that would be fine, I suppose." Assuming we were still living in the house and not the Bronco by then.

"I'd like to take you to lunch," he said. "Why don't you choose a restaurant? Just let me know where, and we can meet there."

"That sounds great," I said, never one to turn down a free lunch.

"Wonderful. Would either Monday or Tuesday of that week be convenient?"

We set up a meeting for Tuesday. And he sounded okay. He had an English accent which I loved. Slap an English accent on even the dimmest of bulbs and they sound intelligent, at least for a while. Not that I thought this Daniel would turn out to be a dim bulb. He sounded quite nice, actually. Julia and I'd had a somewhat rocky relationship, and she'd been losing patience with me. Daniel sounded patient. And he loved my work. If I spent the next three weeks locked in my office, maybe I would actually have something to show him.

The following morning was a stormy one, with wind whipping torrents of rain at the house, and the river dotted with white caps. I knew the roof would soon be leaking. I was staggering around the kitchen attempting to make coffee, when Justin, always the first one up, came clattering down the stairs. He took a loaf of bread out of the bread box, put six slices in the toaster, and finished off the cheerios while he waited for his toast.

Geordie came down next, wearing, as always, his self-imposed uniform. Though he was incredibly picky about his clothes, Geordie was no slave to fashion. He cared nothing about how his clothes looked, but everything about how they felt. He hated wool, denim, nylon, linen, oxford cloth and most combinations thereof. Everything he wore had to be soft cotton or flannel. In the summer he wore tee shirts, plain with no writing or designs, which he said made them itchy, and cotton gym shorts, and in the winter he wore fleece lined running pants and sweat shirts, plain with no writing or designs.

"Mom, I need another leaf. Mr. Baylor said 15 to 20. I have nineteen," Geordie said.

"Well, you have enough then," I told him.

"I really want to have twenty."

"How about a pine needle? We have lots of them."

"Deciduous, Mom. A pine needle is not a deciduous leaf."

"A pine needle is not a deciduous leaf," Justin mocked. "What planet is he from, Mom?"

"He takes his school work seriously. Maybe certain others should take a leaf out of his book. No pun intended."

"Very funny, Mom."

"When is this project due, Geordie?"

"Tomorrow."

"Well, we'll find one," I said, confidently.

Geordie poured himself a bowl of cereal and took a banana from the bowl on the counter.

"Let me slice that for you, sweetie," I said.

"I can do it, Mom."

I took my cup of coffee and sat down at the table. I was in no mood to argue. I just hoped he didn't choose this morning to slice a finger off. Geordie felt that I treated him like a baby. Well, he was six years younger than Justin, and eight younger than Grace.

I looked at the clock. I hadn't heard any noise from upstairs, which meant that Grace was probably still in bed. But, I had to admit, Grace was able to go from fast asleep to out the door in a matter of seconds. Time was an elusive concept for Grace. She saw it as uncertain, uncontrollable, more akin to the weather than to something that could be measured and counted on. She'd never understood that

11

one can actually choose to be in a certain place at a certain time. Finally the kids were off, and I settled down to work, and once again it went well. I drew, and doodled, and a story began to take shape in my mind. I began playing with words, with images. Things were happening; for the first time in years, a story was growing. My worries, the pile of bills on my hall table, my upcoming meeting with Donald Brace at the bank, the leaking roof, all of them blew away like so much charcoal dust on my sketch pad. I was lost in my story and it felt so good I wanted to cry, or to laugh, or to whoop for joy.

It had been Tom who had been the first one to encourage me in my work. He had been my inspiration in so many ways. I would watch him building a boat, watch the way his fingers worked so surely, the knowing way he touched the wood and pride with which he surveyed his finished boats. He got such satisfaction from his work, and he always wanted to sell his boats to buyers who loved them as much as he did. Sometimes he would see one of his boats out on the water, and he would watch it the way a parent surreptitiously watches a child from across the playground. His boats might have gone out into the world, maybe someone else had bought and paid for them, but they were still his.

And, when Tom read my own early offerings, I loved watching his expressions, and I loved hearing him laugh when my characters' antics were funny. It was Tom who had made it all seem possible, not only possible, but inevitable. When he was gone, the possible seemed impossible, and the inevitable seemed irrelevant.

He had been dead for just over three years now. I had been through the stages of grief. First denial. The police were wrong. It wasn't Tom. Even after my sister Emmi had gone with me to identify his crumpled body, I still clung to the belief that it somehow wasn't him.

Then fury. First at the poor truck driver whose rig had killed Tom, and who had somehow emerged himself unhurt. "I'm sorry. I'm so sorry," he kept saying at the funeral, over and over again. Shut up shut up shut the fuck up, I had wanted to scream. I don't care. Who cares if you're sorry? You killed my husband. He's dead. Dead. Do you know what that means? He'll never make love to me again. He'll never take Grace sailing again, or fling Justin over his shoulder and march toward the river, with Justin screaming with laughter and pounding on his back. He'll never give Geordie a piggy back ride, upa da upa da upa da stairs and into da bedidy bedidy bed. He'll never make love to me again. Do you *think* I *care* that you're *sorry?*

And then, anger at Tom. Why had this happened? How had this happened? Was his mind on some stupid frigging boat winch or something that didn't matter one iota when it came to not watching your son play soccer, or your daughter have her first date, or or or.....so, so many things he would miss. So many things I would miss sharing with him, so many things the children would miss not having him there for. And now I had to be both of us, damn him. Who did he think I was? I never fucking wanted to be superwoman. I just wanted to have our life together. With our children. Both doing the things we loved. Too much, I supposed. Too much to ask.

And guilt, of course. Oh yes. Guilt. I was still alive. I could still laugh, hug the children, read books, go for walks, drink wine, eat pancakes, listen to music, call my sister, my friends. I could even forget sometimes, briefly. And sometimes I could even imagine another man, and what it might be like. I was still alive. It hadn't been me. And it hadn't been the children.

And sadness. Deep, deep wells of sadness that would never go away entirely. I missed him. I looked for him all the time. I wanted to tell him about my silly thoughts, my worries, my weird encounters, my memories.

Who else would remember when Grace, aged six, fell and bit her lip on the way to her first dramatic appearance- playing Peter Rabbit's mother- and somehow the two of us together had soothed her and convinced her that a swollen bloody lip would be an asset in that role?

I wanted to see him smile, laugh, nod, understand, the way no one else could possibly understand.

And of course, there was always the "Why me? Why Tom?" which I hated myself for even thinking. I mean, why not me, why not Tom? We had had everything. We had both grown up in supportive families. We had great kids, dear friends, our health, jobs we loved. Compared to most of the human beings on this little planet, who was I to complain? And yet, sometimes I couldn't help but ask, why me, why Tom?

And that was why I needed to work. I needed to work. I needed to work.

A week passed, and I made progress. I was working steadily, harder than I had ever worked before, and a story was coming together.

One morning I remembered the manuscript in my drawer, the one that had jump started my brain. I pulled it out and looked it over. It was as good as I had initially thought. I made some notes and called Louisa Myner. She answered the phone with a tentative 'hello,' as if she were sure it had been a mistake to lift the receiver, but when I told her who I was she warmed up immediately.

"I'm calling to tell you how much I like your manuscript," I explained. "It's lovely. And I think it has a good shot at publication."

"Oh, my," she gasped. "I- I don't know what to say. It's wonderful news."

I told her I'd like to meet with her to talk about it, and we agreed to meet at the Cheshire Cat Café the following Friday afternoon.

The days flew by, and my new book continued to progress. When Friday came and it was time for my meeting with Louisa, I was feeling very pleased. Since I had missed lunch, I decided I would arrive a few minutes early at the Cheshire Cat and have my usual treat, a cappuccino and a blueberry scone. The café was one of my favorite spots, and I had spent many happy hours there. It was bright and cozy, and one wall was painted with a mural of illustrations from *Alice in Wonderland*. My favorite was the one in which the Queen of Hearts is telling Alice, "Sometimes I've believed as many as six impossible things before breakfast."

I spotted Louisa the minute she walked in the door. It was odd, because I'm pretty sure I had never seen her before, and I know I'd never been formally introduced, but somehow I felt as though I'd known her forever. She looked exactly as I had pictured her. She was probably in her early fifties, an attractive, elegant woman, dark hair streaked with grey, pulled back into a chignon, intelligent blue eyes that shone with a light of their own.

She ordered tea and looked around the room. Her manuscript was on the table in front of me, and when she saw it she smiled and came toward me. "Sarah?" she said.

I nodded and stood up to greet her. "Louisa."

She sat down and placed her tea cup carefully on the table in front of her, and then looked at me. "You have made me so happy," she said. "I can't begin to tell you."

I smiled back at her and touched the manuscript lightly with one finger. "It's beautiful," I told her. "I know we can find you a publisher. In fact, I'm going to suggest that you send it to my editor at Pinnacle. His name is Daniel Hollister."

"That would be wonderful," Louisa said.

I wrote out his name and address for her, and explained a little about the publishing business.

Louisa sipped her tea. "This is so kind of you. When I dropped the manuscript off I never dreamed this would happen. I wasn't even certain about taking the class."

"Well, I'm not sure there's much I can teach you. It's clear that you've had plenty of training in painting. Your work is...very accomplished. But I hope you'll take the class. It would be a pleasure to have you there. Are you working on anything else?"

Louisa smiled. I knew that smile. It was a smile that held all the joy and pain and doubt and pleasure an artist feels for a new piece of work. "I am," she said hesitantly. "It's... not much yet. Do you want to see?"

"Of course," I said.

She reached for her bag, flustered. "I was going to wait until class, but I tucked it in at the last minute, in case you asked." I could see her fingers shaking as she drew out her dummy. "This is just a draft. I have a long way to go," she said.

I looked at it quickly. It was, as she said, in its early stages, but I could see that it was going to be as beautiful as *Jesse's Secret*, and I told her so. "Do you mind if I keep this until class? I'd like to give it a more thorough read."

"I'd be honored," she said.

We talked for almost two hours and could have talked more except that I had to leave to pick Geordie up from after-school care.

"So, I'll see you in class a week from Tuesday?" I said, as we stood up.

"You will, indeed," she said. She grasped my hand and said, "Sarah, how can I ever repay you?"

"Believe it or not, you already have," I told her, thinking of my own manuscript on my desk at home.

We went out the door together and had said our goodbyes when she turned back to me. "Oh, and Sarah," she hesitated, as if unsure how to explain, and then went on. "Please don't mention this to anyone. The manuscript, I mean. You see, there's a chance, if your editor does accept it, that I- I may have to publish under a pseudonym. I'm just not certain yet, and I'm not quite ready to go public."

"Of course. I understand completely," I told her, and at the time I thought I did. It seemed logical that she wouldn't want talk about it in class, as if talking about it might somehow jinx the deal. Who hasn't felt that way at some time or another?

I believe that was the only possible clue I had that something wasn't quite right, though I've asked myself again and again if I had missed anything else that day. If I had been more observant, would I have seen sadness behind the light in her eyes, wariness in her glance, or tenseness in her movements? Had I been so caught up in the manuscript that I had missed something? Or had I sought to believe in things that weren't there? Perhaps, like the Queen of Hearts, I was getting too good at believing impossible things.

I stopped by the Arts Center and put Louisa's manuscript in my files there, checked my messages, and went on to pick Geordie up from after school care. On the way home he said, "Evan and Mac and I are starting a business."

"Oh. What kind of business?"

"We're not exactly sure, but Marci Adams and Marissa Alenthorp made $23.00 selling these stupid bead bracelets they made, so we decided we should start a business too."

"Oh. Well, good. I'm all for making money these days."
Geordie didn't say anything for a minute. Then he
asked. "Are we going poor, Mom?"
"Going poor? No, honey. We're just, well, things are a
little tight right now, financially speaking. Why? What
makes you ask that?"
"I heard Grace telling Justin we're going poor, and soon
we'll be broken."
"Going broke, you mean. No. We're not going broke,
and we certainly won't be broken. That's just Grace. You
know how Grace is."
Geordie nodded. "She overacts,"
"Over*reacts*."
"That too," he said.
I laughed. "Oh, Geordie. I'll never be broken as long as I
have you around."
But his words made me wonder. How much did they
know? I thought I had hidden the worst of our financial
situation from them, but kids do have a way of figuring
things out. That night after dinner I realized that Grace, at
least, knew more than I thought she did. Justin was
washing the dishes, by hand, because our dishwasher had
decided now would be a good time to take a little break and
had ceased operation.
"Mom, can't we get this fixed? We need a dishwasher,"
Justin said.
"Oh, I don't know. You seem to be filling the job pretty
well."
"Seriously, Mom, can't we call the appliance guy?"
"We'll see. Let's give it a little time."
"Time? Mom, what, you think it's like, taking a vacation
or something? Dishwashers don't fix themselves, Mom.
They need help."
"Just wash the dishes and shut up, Justin. It's not like
there are that many," Grace said.
"Yeah, right. Just wait till it's your turn," Justin
grumbled.
So Grace knew.

Louisa was up to something-he knew it. He had wasted the whole morning sitting here watching the entrance to her driveway, waiting for her to leave. But he would wait all day long, and all day tomorrow too if he had to, sitting here in this piece-of- shit rental, a tan Buick, as ugly and nondescript as it gets. Well, that's what he needed now. But god, how he hated shit like this. Who designed these things? Had they no taste? No aesthetics? It was sickening. The way this whole fucking country was going. No appreciation for anything beautiful. No understanding of real art, or how an artist works, and why they might fail occasionally. Sickening. Fucking sickening.

Finally he saw her little Honda. She turned left toward town. He put the car in gear and followed, careful to stay far enough behind so that she wouldn't notice him.

He followed her into town, watched her park and go into the cafe. He found a spot across the street and down a bit, and was still there two solid hours later when she came out with another woman. They were both carrying packages, well, large envelopes, really. What the hell was that? Not paintings surely. Too small for that. The women chatted for a minute- seemed very lovey-dovey- the way women are- and then parted. Who was that woman? What the hell business did Lou have with her?

She was up to something, Louisa was, and he intended to find out what.

He watched the other woman walk across the street to the Arts Center and disappear inside. He drove to the Center parking lot, pulled into a far corner and prepared to wait. Had Lou mentioned anyone? A new friend, or... not that she would tell him. Not anymore.

Finally he saw the woman walk through the lot and climb into a large maroon Bronco. He followed her out of the lot, back through town, and god help him, to the fucking school. Jesus, he pulled off to the side- a school was just what he needed- talk about how to look like a freak, parking in a school lot and no kid to pick up.

But soon a kid came out and climbed into the Bronco, and then, after she waved to the frigging teacher and strapped the kid in, they finally got underway. Thank god

*she seemed to be heading home finally- out the Peach
Blossom Road to Starlings Neck.*

*When she turned onto an unpaved road- Jesus- why not
pave the frigging road- he followed, but he was worried-
was it a dead end? This may have been a mistake. But then
she turned into a driveway, and he made a note of the
address and went on up the road and found a place to turn
around. As he drove past her place again he slowed down
to get a look at the license number of her car. Might come in
handy sometime.*

*Then he headed back to the crap motel where he was
staying. It was ridiculous, staying in a shithole like that, but
what choice did he have? He didn't want Lou to know he
was here yet. And let's face it, funds were tight, and from
the way Lou was acting it didn't seem like things would be
getting better anytime soon. Especially if he had to keep
shelling out for rental cars and crap motels.*

*How many times had he told her to keep a low profile?
And it wasn't as if she didn't want to anyway. She hated
the limelight, hated socializing, publicity. Hell, if it hadn't
been for him god knows what would have happened to her.
This is what she just didn't get. How much she needed him.
So much more than he needed her, really, though she'd
never admit it.*

*He decided it was time to confront her. He'd go talk to
her tonight and find out what she was up to.*

Chapter Three

A few days after my meeting with Louisa I was in my office in the Arts Center when I got a call from Justin.

"Mom, there's something wrong with Paddington," he said, sounding frantic.

"What do you mean, Jus?"

"She's like, she can hardly walk. And she's like, really out of it. She's sick, Mom. She's really sick."

Paddington had a stomach like a trash compacter. She was never sick.

"She must've gotten into something. I'll be right home," I told him, already hurrying out to my car.

A few minutes later I turned off Peach Blossom Road onto the unpaved sandy lane that led to our house. On the right side of the lane was an ancient barn, picturesque in spite of its dilapidation, surrounded by fields of soybeans and cattle corn. On the left side, beyond the green swath of lawns which gave way to marsh grass and needle rush, and just visible between the cedar and locust trees on her bank, the river glistened in the afternoon sun. Ours was the third of the five houses on the lane; a comfortable old farmhouse shaded by oaks and elms and one glorious magnolia tree, presiding over all.

Paddington was lying under the magnolia tree. Justin knelt beside her, cradling her head in his lap, and offering her water from his sports bottle. Together we managed to lift her into the backseat of the car.

"Got into some poison, would be my guess," our vet, Heidi Tillard said, as she examined her. "She'll be pretty woozy for a day or two. Keep a close eye on her." She drew blood, gave her some injections, and gave us instructions for her care. "Once I run the blood work I might be able to tell you more precisely what caused it."

We loaded her back in the car and headed for home, stopping on the way to pick Geordie up from after school care. Naturally Geordie was the one who first noticed that something was amiss once we got home.

"Look, Mom. The back door's open," he said as we helped Paddington to her favorite spot on the back porch.

Inside there was chaos. Most of the drawers and cabinets in the house had been ransacked, and my office had been turned upside down.

"When did this happen?" I asked, stunned. "Was it like this when you got home, Jus?"

He shrugged. "I didn't go inside. I didn't want to leave Paddington. I called you as soon as I saw she was sick, and then I waited with her."

We called the police and took a quick inventory. Bizarrely, nothing seemed to be missing. We were still staring helplessly at the mess when Grace arrived home.

"What happened?" she asked.

We went over the whole thing again, and Grace raced upstairs to access the damage to her own room. Fortunately, not too much had been disturbed in any of the kids' rooms.

The police came- well- a police came. Officer Shanihan, a middle aged, overweight man with purple bags under his tired eyes. He studied the crime scene for about five minutes, made some notes, put bits of "evidence" in a plastic bag, and scratched his head in perplexity. "Nothing taken? You're sure?"

"We haven't found anything missing so far," I said.

"You keep any drugs in the house?"

"Drugs?"

"It's possible they were looking for drugs. Possibly vandals, kids on a lark."

21

"We think they poisoned our dog," Geordie told him. He had been listening to every word the man said, and taking notes himself, as if he were the one doing the investigating. Officer Shanihan nodded. "I'm aware of that, son." He looked at me and held out his card. "You give me a call when you hear the results of the blood work. Or if any more information surfaces, anything turns up missing. I'll do some checking, talk to the neighbors. I'll be in touch."

He left. We ordered pizza and began cleaning up. Geordie and Justin lasted till the pizza arrived. Grace hung in there for another few minutes, until her phone rang, and she disappeared, taking a slice of pizza and her cell phone with her.

A few days after the break in I learned from Heidi Tillard that Paddington had ingested enough tranquilizers to render her almost unconscious for several hours. They were wearing off when Justin found her at 3:30, so she must have ingested them early in the day. I reported as much to Officer Shanihan, who told me that, so far, none of the neighbors had noticed a stranger around, or an unusual car on the lane. The findings from the "evidence" were inconclusive, but the investigation was proceeding. I had completed the clean up, and Paddington was feeling her old self again, and I went on working like Rumpelstiltskin on my new book.

And then the day came for my meeting with Daniel Hollister. What to wear? I didn't want to wear my suit-too formal- but my usual jeans were definitely not appropriate. I realized as I stared into my closet that I was nervous. Very nervous. I had only had two different editors in my whole twelve years with Pinnacle. The first, Denise Comstock, had been my favorite. Julia Zemeron had taken over from Denise two years ago. Julia and I were not as compatible, so I was not particularly sad that Daniel was replacing her.

After pulling out and rejecting several different outfits, I finally settled on my good black skirt, an old favorite, and a silk tank and matching sweater in a great shade of coral.

I hadn't bought a new pair of shoes in months, so I raided Grace's closet and found a pair that were probably way too old fashioned for her, but worked okay for me.

When I got it all together, it looked pretty good. I put on some make up, tamed my hair as best I could, and finally, looking in the mirror one last time, I decided I was as ready as I'd ever be.

I parked in the back parking lot of the Arts Center and walked around front to the entrance where we had agreed to meet. A pleasant-looking man was sitting on a bench reading the paper, and when I stopped in the door to the center, he stood and came over to me.

"Mrs. Landing," he said, holding out his hand. "I'm Daniel Hollister."

We shook hands and I said, "It's Sarah. I'm so happy to meet you, Daniel." He was dressed in a beautifully cut brown suit with a beige linen shirt, open at the neck, no tie, a New York editor's idea of Eastern Shore business casual, I guessed.

"I recognized you from your publicity photos," he said, smiling, "though I must say they don't do you justice. The photos are very attractive, but not a patch on the real thing." This might have sounded cheesy, but his English accent made it work somehow.

"How was your trip?" I asked.

"Lovely. This is my first time in this part of the world. It's beautiful."

"It is, isn't? Did you come from New York this morning?"

"I was in Washington yesterday. I spent last night with an old friend in Bethesda and drove over this morning," he explained. "I parked in the lot in back of the Arts Center. Is that okay?"

"Fine. Mine's there too." I waved in the direction of the Galley. "Our restaurant is just a few blocks down. Shall we walk?"

"Absolutely," he said, and he fell into step beside me.

"How was the traffic?" I asked. "It can be terrible on the bridge sometimes. Of course, it's worse on the weekends."

"It wasn't bad at all. That's why I was early. I'd been forewarned, but the traffic failed to materialize, so I had a bit of a stroll around town."

"It must seem a sleepy backwater compared to New York," I said.

23

"It's charming. Reminds me a bit of my hometown in England."

"It is pretty," I agreed. "Especially this time of year."

We arrived at the Galley and were seated on the deck overlooking the river.

A waiter appeared and rattled off the specials. When we had given him our order, Daniel said, "I know this is supposed to be a business lunch, but it's so beautiful here, and I'd like to toast to our new working relationship. What do you say to some wine?"

"I will if you will," I told him. After all, it was a beautiful day, and I had worked hard for the last few weeks.

When he had ordered the wine he said, "You were at Bradbury House Publishers before Pinnacle, weren't you?"

I nodded, impressed. He had definitely done his homework. "They published my first book, now long out of print. I was grateful to them for taking a chance on me, but it wasn't a good match. My editor there drove me crazy. He was always quoting marketing. Marketing says this, marketing says that. It made me want to hit him over the head with my story board."

"Hmmm." He mimed writing a note on his palm. "Note to self-be prepared to flee should the subject of marketing arise."

I smiled. "Not to worry. I never actually hit him. I just thought about it."

The waiter appeared with our food, and we spent the next few minutes tasting and commenting. Then he got back to business. "*A Dog's Life* and *A Cat's Life* sold very well."

"Yes."

There was a pause, both of us waiting for the other to continue. Finally I said, "But please don't suggest *A Hamster's Life* or *A Gold Fish's Life*." I was only half joking. Julia had actually suggested both.

"But marketing says-" he joked.

I laughed, and he filled my wine glass. The sun sparkled on the water, and for a few minutes I forgot about everything and took pleasure in the beautiful day and the delicious lunch.

He sipped his wine, fiddled with his fork and said, "Julia told me about your husband."

"Mm."

"I'm-I'm very sorry. It must have been..." He closed his eyes and shook his head slightly.

"Yes. It was. "

"She also said you have three children. Tell me about them."

So I did, and he told me about his son, Ian. "Small for his age, thoughtful, oddly self- contained for a twelve year old. I adore him," he said simply, and I could see in his eyes that it was true.

I asked about his wife.

"We're divorced," he said. "It's been five years now. We have joint custody, and it seems to be working. Ian is with me half the time, and seems okay with the situation."

We had finished eating and were drinking coffee when he said, "Julia also mentioned that your new book is progressing, uh, more slowly than had been hoped?"

I smiled. "I'll be honest with you. The new book was pretty much nonexistent until a few weeks ago. I just couldn't seem to get anything started. At least, nothing worth keeping. Then, something happened, and I've been working steadily ever since. I actually have something I'm pretty pleased with. It's got a long way to go, of course, but it's happening."

He studied my face as if gauging my sincerity. Then he said, "Wonderful. When can I see it?"

"Well, right now, if you like. We can go back to my place and I'll show it to you."

He paid our bill, and we walked back to the Arts Center.

"Why don't I follow you in my car?" he said. "That way you won't have to bring me back to town."

"All right. That sounds fine." I was relieved. My car was littered with dog hair, sports equipment and old MacDonald's bags. I didn't want his beautiful suit to be subjected to it.

As I drove home with Daniel behind me, I had an attack of nerves. What if I had been fooling myself? What if my new book was terrible? It was way too early to show him.

25

This was a huge mistake. By the time I pulled into our driveway, I was a wreck.

Daniel pulled in behind me. "This is beautiful," he said, as he got out of the car and looked around. "What a view!"

"Yes. The house was a mess when we bought it. A serious fixer-upper. It took us forever. But the view is worth it all."

"Are your children home?" he asked, checking his watch.

"No. Geordie has after school care until five, Justin has soccer practice, and Grace has driver's Ed." I lead him up to my office babbling on that way about how rough the new book was, not really ready, yadda yadda.

I had several sketches on my easels, a storyboard, and a dummy with a rough text laid out. He smiled when he saw the sketches, and I took heart.

"Would you mind if I take a few minutes to look these over?" he asked.

"Not at all. Please sit down. I- I've got some calls to make, so I'll leave you to it, if that's okay."

He looked relieved. There's nothing worse than trying to read someone's work when they're hanging over your shoulder.

"Perfect. I won't be long," he said.

In the kitchen I took several deep breaths, almost causing myself to hyperventilate. This was a terrible mistake. Why had I let him see it? What was I thinking? I sat down, stroking Paddington and pretending to be busy making lists. Finally I heard him on the steps.

"Sarah," he called.

I went to the door of the kitchen. He was smiling broadly. "In here, Daniel."

"It's terrific! I love it!" he said.

I let out a sigh of relief. "Really? You liked it?"

"Very much. It's quite different, of course, from your other work. But there's nothing wrong with that. I'm very impressed."

"Well, it's got a long way to go," I said. "It's still very rough."

"Of course. The thing is, I don't want to rush you, but our spring list is kind of slight right now. I'd love to perk it up. If we rush production, we could make it if we get your completed manuscript by, say, the end of November?"

"November?"

"I'm, um, I'm prepared to offer you another advance. I think we could go as high as, say $20,000. Of course, I'll have to get it cleared, but I'm pretty confident I can get it."

"T-Twenty thousand?"

"And that again when we get the manuscript in November, of course."

Twenty thousand? This was a gift from heaven. That money could save us. I'd be able to pay the mortgage and still have enough left to tide us over. It was the answer to my prayers.

"And I can guarantee that we will get behind this book. Sales could be...well, it could be big."

"Yes. Yes," I said quickly before he came to his senses and changed his mind. "I can have more for you in say, um, a month, and I can finish it by mid November. I- I'm sure of it."

"Great," he said. "I'll get the paperwork to Katharine Briggs, and you should have your check in a few weeks. I'm very excited about this, Sarah. From what I've seen I think it can be big."

"I'm just so happy you like it," I said.

"I hope you won't hold it against me that I'm rushing you like this."

Hold it against him? I would never hold anything against this man. He was my savior. He believed in my work. He was giving me money. I could have leapt across the counter and kissed him right then and there.

"Oh," I said, remembering Louisa Myner's manuscript. "I have something else I wanted to mention. A manuscript, not mine, but one belonging to a student. It's beautiful. It's called *Jesse's Secret*. It's about a little boy who befriends a homeless man and helps him get back on his feet."

"*Jesse's Secret*. I love the title. Tell your friend to send it to me," he said.

I was about to tell him that I had already done so when the cheery tinny tune that Grace had programmed into my cell phone sounded. The phone was in my purse on the kitchen counter. My purse was a large one, and it had a habit of getting bigger, bottomless actually, whenever I was looking for something in it. As the ringing continued and I began to panic, the bag grew to gargantuan proportions. I was half way inside it, and bits of paper, fuzzy lifesavers and other detritus from its depths were flying around when I finally got my hand on the phone, which promptly stopped ringing. I pulled it out and checked the number. Geordie's school.

"Uh oh," I said.

"A problem?" he asked.

"Possibly," I told him. "It's my son's school."

I hit return call and reached Janine, the school nurse. "Oh, Mrs. Landing. Thank heavens."

"What's happened?" I asked.

"Geordie's had a bit of an accident. He's okay," she said quickly, "but I'm afraid he may have broken his arm. He'll need an x-ray. And he's in quite a bit of pain. Can you come?"

"Yes. I'll come right away."

"We'll be waiting right here in my office."

"I'm on my way."

I told Daniel what had happened. "I'll have to go right over to the school. I'm so sorry."

"I am too. Can I do anything to help?"

"Thank you, but I just have to pick him up and get him to the doctor's. Can you find your way back to Rt. 50?"

"Certainly." He grabbed his coat and followed me out the door.

"I'm so sorry about this," I said.

"Of course I understand. Don't give it another thought."

"It was so nice of you to come all the way down here."

"My pleasure. I'll be in touch from New York. It was lovely to meet you."

"It was. And thank you for lunch," I said stopping long enough to shake hands with him.

In the nurse's office, Geordie sat slumped in a chair looking tiny and stunned, like a baby bird who had fallen out of the nest. He was cradling one arm, and I could see that he had been crying. When he saw me his eyes filled

28

again, and I felt close to tears myself, though I knew that a broken arm was not that serious in the scheme of things.

"Oh, baby. What happened?" I knelt beside his chair and put my arms around him, being careful not to squeeze his injured arm.

"I fell off the jungle gym," he said through his tears. "It hurts, Mom."

"Of course it does, honey. But we'll get you to Dr. Fletcher, and he'll fix you up."

Janine came in from the next room. "Here's Mom. Good grief, she must have rented a helicopter to get here so fast." She smoothed back the hair on Geordie's forehead. "He has been such a brave fellow. And I know how it hurts. I broke my wrist once, and I'll tell you, you could hear me hollering all the way over in Dorchester County."

Geordie managed a little smile.

"I gave him some Tylenol-that's all we can do here. Where will you take him for the x-ray?"

"I called Hank Fletcher. He said to bring him right in."

Hank Fletcher was a bone doctor, and also a friend and had set the limbs of half the children in town.

"Good," Janine said with a nod. "He's the best."

"Yes." I took Geordie's good hand and he stood up. "Come on, sweetie. Let's get you to Dr. Fletcher's. I looked at Janine. "Do I need to sign him out or anything?"

"Just take him, poor guy. I'll do the rest."

I thanked Janine and got Geordie to Hank Fletcher's office, where he confirmed that the wrist was indeed broken.

I held Geordie's hand while Hank set the bone and put a cast on it. It was just a broken bone. A bone that could be fixed, and made good as new. That was all. Nothing more. As Hank worked, I watched Geordie's small face. I studied every line and shadow of those beloved features. How fragile they were, he was, we all were. And how infinitely precious.

I was so lost in my thoughts that I jumped when Hank said, "There we are. He's a tough guy. He'll be good as new in a few weeks." He gave us instructions and a prescription, and sent Geordie off with the nurse to pick out a good patient prize from the box of little toys they kept for these occasions.

He gave the guy cash for the boat rental. Lucky he had gotten plenty of cash before he came back here. Didn't want to leave a paper trail. He hopped into the pram and started the piddly little motor. It was still early, barely light yet, so there weren't many boats out, just a few watermen and one or two early morning sailors.

It would take him at least half an hour to get there in this tub, but he had to do it. He couldn't risk being seen, and he wouldn't be seen if he played his cards right. He had to get the key to that Arts Center. The second manuscript had to be in there. It wasn't in her house, so it had to be in her office in the Center. He should have thought of that before he had gone into her house, but that had been pretty easy. They hadn't even locked the house then, before the break in, which technically wasn't even a break in since he had just walked right in through the unlocked door. Except for the dog. That had made things a bit more complicated, but the xanax in the meat ball had taken care of that. That had been smart.

He had spent the yesterday morning scoping out the situation at the Center and had realized he would have to go in after dark, after the place was locked up, which meant he had to have a key. It wasn't open to the public until eleven, but it seemed like half the town had keys to the place, and came and went as they pleased. He had watched Sarah- that was her name- Sarah Landing- unlock the door of the place at around ten am, and had seen the bright orange plastic fob with two keys on it that she had used. Then she had tucked it back in her purse, where, presumably, it was still waiting for him.

He steered the little boat up Peach Blossom until he was just around the bend from her house and opposite a wooded bit of shore that was out of sight from any house. Then he cut the engine, pulled the motor up, took out an oar and poled himself to shore.

He grabbed his backpack which held his binoculars, a sandwich, a thermos of coffee, and a book, and climbed out of the boat. He pulled it up farther on shore, found a spot

30

that was hidden from the water and from the road, and tied the painter to a felled tree. Then he set out through the woods toward the house.

When he was close enough to have a good view, but still hidden, he found a log and sat down, prepared to wait until she went out with the dog. He'd been watching her for a few days now, ever since he had followed Louisa and found out about the book. Louisa had told him about the class Sarah taught at the Arts Center-the class that Lou had been planning to take- and he had gotten a schedule and found out what time she taught. And he had watched her house, too, from his car and from the woods near the house, but he couldn't risk coming by car anymore. He liked watching them though. Same way he had liked watching Lou. Too bad. Too bad about Lou. But it was her own fault. All her own fault.

He poured himself a cup of coffee, took out the binoculars and watched. It was kind of like watching a play, or a TV show.

The sky was beginning to lighten in the east. They would be up soon, he thought, and then he saw the first light blink on in one of the upstairs rooms. Then a hall light, and the kitchen light. The door opened, dog out, paper in. He hadn't really needed to be here this early, but he hadn't wanted to risk having anyone see him pulling the boat up on shore. He ate his sandwich, then took out his book, keeping one eye on the house.

It was mid-morning and the kids had long since left when he finally got his chance. He saw her come out of the house, whistle for the dog, and head off down the road, leaving the house open and her purse inside. Just as he had hoped.

He waited a few minutes, making sure she was really gone, then hurried to the house. The door was unlocked as he knew it would be. What a ditz. Did she need him to send a telegram? Jesus.

And there was her purse, right in plain sight sitting on a chair in the kitchen. He grabbed it, pulled out her wallet, car keys, checkbook, healthy snack bar- of course- and then, finally his fingers closed on the plastic fob that held the keys he needed. He pocketed them, shoved her stuff back into the purse, put it back exactly where he'd found it, and got the hell out of there.

Chapter Four

On Tuesday night I arrived a few minutes early to prepare for the first session of my new class. I had gone in early to the Arts Center the day before because I wanted to spend some time going over Louisa's new manuscript and thinking about it before I gave it back to her with my comments in class.

This draft had only one water color, a few sketches, and the outline of a story, but it was more than enough to see that it was going to be lovely, and the art was in the same distinctive style as *Jesse's Secret*. The storyline was not as strong- which was understandable given that it was a draft, and I had to admit feeling slightly pleased that I would be able to help her get it in shape, and that she wouldn't be wasting her time in my class.

I fetched the draft from my files, along with some notes and some picture books I wanted to share, and went down to the classroom.

I arranged my books, readied my notes, put eleven handout packets on eleven desks, and waited for my students. I was always a bit nervous before a first class, nervous and curious. Even though I had taught the course so many times before, every class was different, like a new production of an old play.

I liked teaching at the Arts Center because my students were adults, and they had chosen to be there and to take the class. Of course, there was always a wide variety of skill levels. There were the ones who were only there because the scrap booking class or the French cooking class was full. And there were the occasional oddballs: the interrupter, the arguer, the sigher, and most bizarre of all, the rocker, who rocked back and forth in her seat for the duration of the class. Over the years, though, most of my students had been interesting, likeable people that I had enjoyed knowing, and many of them were serious artists and writers.

At a few minutes before seven my first student appeared shyly in the open doorway.

"Is this room 34? The Art of the Picture Book?"

"It is indeed. I'm Sarah Landing. Come in and find a seat. You're the first one here, so you get first choice."

"Well, I'll sit front and center. Right under your nose. That way I can't get into any trouble."

I smiled. She was an older woman, in her sixties I guessed, with stylishly cut white hair, and piercing brown eyes. Other students were filing in and finding seats. There was an older man in a flannel shirt and chinos, a middle aged man in a business suit who looked as if he just stepped out of a board meeting. Two youngish women, late twenties or earlier thirties. Two women with beautiful coffee colored skin, one young, and one older came in together. Mother and daughter as it turned out, hoping to collaborate.

But no Louisa Myner.

At seven o'clock I stood up and walked around my desk, signaling that it was time to get started. The class progressed from there, and continued without disruption, and, to my disappointment, without Louisa Myner, until nine o'clock when class was over.

It had gone well, and I was pleased overall, but disappointed that Louisa, who would undoubtedly be my most talented student, had not shown. I dropped her draft back in my file and left the center wondering why she hadn't been there.

When I got home there was the usual post-dinner chaos in the kitchen. Someone, probably Grace, had made an attempt at washing the dishes, but had apparently gotten interrupted or sidetracked. There were still dishes in the sink, and the dish washer was half full and open, waiting to be fed. I finished them up and then went upstairs to read to Geordie and tuck him into bed. Finally I had a minute to listen to my phone messages and check my e-mail, thinking that maybe Louisa had left a message explaining her absence, or saying that she had changed her mind about taking my class, but there was nothing.

The following day I called my friend Connie Mather, Director of Education at the Arts Center and asked if Louisa Myner had withdrawn from my class.

"Nope. Still registered. Maybe she got sick. She'll probably turn up next week."

"Yes. That's probably what happened. Thanks, Connie."

Once he had the key, getting into the place was easy. He knew Sarah was teaching her first class that Tuesday night. He knew she would check for it before the class, and he didn't want to alarm her by taking it before that. Why put thoughts into anyone's head? He waited till one AM, plenty late enough. This wasn't New York City. In this town you'd be lucky to find a cat awake at that hour.

Driving through town in his rented piece of crap was weird. There was no one out. No one. A Tuesday night in the town of the dull and the boring.

He parked in the Arts Center parking lot, making sure his car was not visible from the street- some cop might be roaming- although from what he'd seen of them they were all as sound asleep as the citizens. Dreaming of sugar plums, as Lou would have said. Damn. He didn't want to think about her now. He had to focus.

He went to the back door, pulled out the keys, tried the big one which worked. The other one must be for her office. He put them back in his pocket and went inside.

He was surprised at the size of the place. Well, not size, it wasn't that big, but there were a lot of rooms. Class rooms, a sort of gallery type space, and then offices. Two floors. He had a flashlight but should he use it? He decided he would have to- some of the offices had names, but most didn't. There were no windows in the hall, so he decided he was safe with it.

He shined his light on the office doors. No Sarah Landing. Seven or eight doors without names. He would just have to try them all.

He tried five and was getting ready to bomb the fucking place when finally his key opened the sixth door. Frankly, he was kind of surprised the ditz had bothered to lock it.

He waved the beam of his flashlight around the tiny office. No window, he could turn on the light. He shut the door and flipped the light switch. He checked the desk, hoping the thing might be sitting there, waiting for him, but no such luck. He would have to tackle the files. Good thing he'd remembered to wear gloves. He started on the files. Jesus, there was a lot of shit in there. Past classes, lectures, handouts, ahh. Student work- yes. There it was. A large envelop,-New Pic. Book- Untitled in Lou's handwriting. He opened the envelop and checked just in case and there was one of her watercolors, unmistakably hers. He resisted the urge to go through the whole. Later. For now he had to get out of there, making sure he left no signs that he or anyone had been here.

He put everything back just as it had been, turned out the light, locked both doors. Then he drove out to Starlings neck , parked down the road from the house, and made his way to the driveway. He left the key fob on the ground near the driver's side of the car. The ditz would think she had dropped it there after her class. He didn't want her to know anyone had borrowed it. And he sure wouldn't want to cause her the trouble of a lost key now would he? What a nice guy he was.

Chapter Five

Over the next week I called and e-mailed Louisa several more times, but never got an answer. The week passed, another class came and went, and still she didn't show.

Finally, when I hadn't heard from her by the end of the second week of my class, I decided to drive out to her house to see her.

She had told me she lived in a small cottage with a view of the Tred Avon. I had her address on the card she had given me, and I knew it would take only about ten minutes to drive over there.

I hadn't been out that way in years, and driving down Hopkins Neck I was surprised to see how much building had gone on. There were several new developments since I had been there last. It was the middle of the afternoon and the streets had a deserted feeling; the houses looking sleepy and bored, as if they were waiting for their families to come home. Farther down Hopkins Neck, the development ended and gave way to woods and fields.

Louisa rented a small cottage on the grounds of an old manor house. Most of the property had been sold off, and there were only about three acres left. The road that led to the manor house and the cottage was a sandy lane bordered on both sides by two perfect rows of cedar trees. The cottage itself was small and cozy looking, and did indeed have a great view of the Tred Avon River.

I parked in her drive way, walked up to the door and knocked.

I waited a few minutes and knocked again. A dog was barking, but whether it was from inside the house or elsewhere I couldn't tell. I knocked one more time, feeling extremely frustrated. I wanted to talk to her. It was so rare that I was able to be so positive about a manuscript. And besides, though I had only met her the one time, I liked her, and I'd had the feeling we could be friends.

Finally, worried that I was quickly falling into the stalker category, I gave up. I wrote her a quick note imploring her to call me and left it inside the screen door.

As I was heading back down the lane, a car was coming towards me, and because the lane was so narrow, I stopped and pulled off to the side to let it pass. I wondered if he was going to Louisa's house too. As he drove slowly by he waved to thank me for pulling over, and I got a good look at him. He had longish gray hair pulled back in a ponytail, and wore what looked to be Armani, which was odd, because most of the good old boys on the Eastern Shore think Armani is a kind of brandy. Must be an import from DC, I decided, probably visiting Louisa's landlords.

In a small community like Easton, news travels fast. Geordie had already heard about it when I picked him up from after school care, though I didn't realize it at the time. I pulled up in front of his school and saw him waiting for me just inside the doors, his back pack on, ready to go. When he saw me he gave an abrupt little wave and shouted over his shoulder to his teacher, Mrs. Eldridge that I was here. Mrs. Eldridge appeared in the doorway and waved. She gave Geordie a hug and sent him out the door. He raced down the steps and climbed into the car.

"Hi, sweetie," I said, leaning over to kiss him.

"Hi, Mom," he said. He let me kiss him and then collapsed against the seat and let out a loud sigh. "Man. Benjy's lucky."

"How so?" I asked.

"He found a dead body, and now he gets to be on the news."

"Benjy found a dead body?"

"Yup. He said it was gross."

"Are you sure he isn't just making up stories, Geordie?" I asked.

"Nope. He's going to be on the news tonight. Definitely."

"Well, if Benjy's going to be on I guess we'll have to watch," I said. Geordie's friend Benjy Mitchell was known for his overactive imagination. I didn't for a minute think he had actually found a dead body.

"So what else happened today?" I asked.

"We had a math test. It was hard. And we're making masks in art. See you have this goopy stuff and you put it on your face."

He launched into a detailed discussion of the mask making operation to which I listened with half an ear.

Justin was already home when we got there, in his usual position halfway into the fridge.

"No practice today?" I asked.

"Cancelled. Coach is out."

I hit the voice mail to listen to my messages. The usual fare, a telemarketer informing me that today was my lucky day, the plumber, wondering if I had sent payment for his last two visits, a call from Connie, which I would return after dinner.

We were having chicken breasts for dinner, and as I took them out of the package and began to cut them up, I noticed Geordie watching me carefully. "What's up, hon?" I asked.

"Nothing," he said, continuing to stand beside me.

I put my knife down and began to put the chicken pieces in the pan. "Mom. Did you know that chicken has bacteria?"

"Yes. That's why you cook it. The heat kills the bacteria," I said.

"But on the news I watched this chicken inspector. He went into people's kitchens and found out that they were poisoning their families."

"What?"

"It's true. This one lady put her knife down like you just did and he said that would probably make her family sick."

"A chicken inspector came into people's houses? Geordie, that can't be right."

"It's true, Mom," Grace called from the sunroom where she was setting the table. "I saw the thing he's talking about. It was one of those news- cam- two- investigates."

Geordie nodded. "You have to wash your hands and utensils every time they touch the chicken."

"God, it's not enough to have everyone scared to death about terrorism. Now they have to dream up death by chicken. That channel specializes in terrorizing people," I said.

"Well, it's lucky I saw that program," Geordie told me. "You don't want us to get sick, do you, Mom?"

"No, sweetie. It is lucky. Now we have our very own chicken inspector." I washed the knife and my hands while Geordie nodded approval.

Just what I needed- the chicken Gestapo. Thank you news- cam- two.

I snapped the TV off before we saw any more horror stories.

"But, Mom. You have to leave it on. Benjy's going to be on."

"Not during dinner, Geordie. If Benjy's on the news I'm sure he'll tape it and let you see it."

We had just sat down to dinner when the phone rang. "Let the machine get it," I said, but Justin had already grabbed it.

"Yo?" he said, and then, "Just a sec, Connie. She's right here," He held the phone out to me. "It's Connie. She says it's important."

"Sarah, did you see the news?" she asked.

"No, why?"

"You know that student you were asking me about?"

"Louisa Myner?"

"Yes. Louisa Myner. So- you haven't heard?"

"Heard what?" I was getting impatient, and my dinner was getting cold.

"She's dead. Sheila Mitchell's boys found her body washed up on the beach out near Thomas point.

Chapter Six

Louisa Myner was dead. That much was known, but according to Connie, very little else about the situation was. When my shock receded and I was able to speak, I pelted her with questions. How? When? Where, and of course, the big one, why? There was nothing she could tell me, and although we turned the news on immediately, and did indeed see Benjy Mitchell and his brother Tim, pointing to the spot where they had discovered the body, there was not much more information to be gleaned that night.

The next morning we heard that a small row boat had been found washed up not far from the body, and, according to police, it was similar to one that allegedly belonged to Louisa Myner. Police were still looking into the matter, but at this point, it looked to be a boating accident that had sent Louisa to a watery grave.

How sad the whole thing was. Sad that she had died in this pointless way. Sad that she had died alone, and had not been missed for several days. And how unutterably sad that she had not lived to see her book in print. I vowed that I would make sure her family, assuming she had some family, knew about it, and that I would help them get it published.

In the meantime, I was determined that I would not let Louisa's death set me back. It was the least I could do for this woman whose own manuscript had rekindled the

41

spark in me. I owed it to her, to my kids, to myself, and of course, to Tom.

Tom's real gifts to me were, of course, Grace, Justin and Geordie, and I knew as surely as I knew anything, that they needed me to get on with my work, to show them that life goes on, and that we can make meaning out of chaos. It was for them, and for Tom, that I had been working harder and accomplishing more than I ever had in so short a time.

The morning of my meeting with Donald Brace, the mortgage banker was cold and stormy. A northeast wind had blown in overnight, bringing with it pelting rain. My meeting was scheduled for ten o'clock. By the time the kids left for school I still had more than two hours before I had to be there, which was good, because I didn't want to be harassed and rushed when I arrived. I wanted to be calm and collected, on time and in control. I would shower and dress carefully, and I would look poised and confident when I arrived at his office.

As I was finishing the breakfast dishes I made a mental note to dig my good umbrella out of the back hall closet. That was when I noticed that the garbage can Grace was supposed to have put away in the garage last night had blown over and was rolling down the driveway. I rushed outside and caught it just before it got to the road.

Lugging it back up the drive, in my bathrobe and slippers, I saw that the front door had blown shut behind me. Since the break-in I had instigated a policy of locking the doors. We had never been diligent about locking up before, but I had decided it was time we started. Not that there was much worth stealing from our house, but still, it seemed irresponsible not to lock the doors. I had given everyone a key, and had hidden several others in strategic locations outside. When I saw the door shut I knew that it was locked, but I wasn't worried. This was precisely why I had hidden other keys around the yard.

One key was hidden under a stone by the back door. I had checked to make sure it was still there last week. I put the can back in the garage and went around to the back of the house and checked for it. No key. At this point I felt a spasm of irritation, but I remained calm, comforted by the fact that I had hidden another extra key in the bird feeder, and I had given another one to my neighbor if all else failed. I trooped to bird feeder and felt for the key. Not there. Now I was seriously irritated, but not yet panicked. My terrycloth bathrobe was soaked through, and the fuzzy, florescent purple slippers I had inherited from Grace were sodden sponge-like clumps, each of which now weighed approximately ten pounds. I marched down the road to the Sweeney's house and rang the doorbell.

Marty and Skip Sweeny had moved to the Shore from Baltimore about a year before. Skip, an accountant, had opened a small branch office of his firm in Easton. Marty was originally from South Carolina. She was younger than me by maybe five years or so, and had two small children who seemed to be on a constant sugar high. Maybe I'd just forgotten what small kids were like, but two minutes with these two and I needed medication. And the more wound up they got, the calmer Marty got.

Marty answered the door and didn't seem in the least bit surprised to see me dripping on her doorstep in my bathrobe and sodden slippers.

"Hey, Sarah," she drawled. "C'mon in. Want a cup of coffee? I have a few minutes before I have to get Jimmy and Carol to preschool."

"Thanks, Marty, but I just need my key. I'm locked out, and I'm going to be late for a meeting if I don't hurry."

"Oh, dear."

"I'm so sorry for bothering you, but thank heavens I left that spare with you."

"But, Sarah, honey. I don't have your key anymore. I gave it to Justin a few days ago."

"What?"

"Did that little rascal forget to tell you?"

A mental image of Justin's backpack flashed before my eyes. There was a clinking sound coming from it. The kind of clinking sound that would be made by keys.

Fury washed over me like a red tide.

There was a shriek from the kitchen and Marty took my arm and guided me gently inside. "You want to use the phone, hon?"

43

Rage and shock had rendered me temporarily unable to speak.

"Let me go check on those minxes, and then we'll think what to do."

When she came back I said, "Can you give me a ride down to the school?"

"Why sure, hon, but…" She looked at my coffee stained bathrobe and the fluorescent sponges on my feet.

"Could I borrow a raincoat or something?" Marty was only about five feet tall and weighed probably 160. I was five six and weighed 130. Borrowing her clothes was out of the question, but a coat would do. "Just anything. I have to find Justin." I wanted my house keys, of course, but more than that I wanted Justin's head. On a plate. With an apple in his mouth.

Even the unflappable Marty grasped the fact that my emotional state was moving in to the danger zone. She rustled in the closet and came out with a long belted trench coat. This is Skip's, but you're welcome to borrow it. And, let's see, what size shoe are you?"

"7 1/2," I told her.

"Hmmm. These might do. I'm only a six, but these are kind of big." They were hideous, a fashion don't, without a doubt, but better than soggy purple slippers. I squeezed my feet into them, donned the trench coat and we were ready to go.

Marty herded the children into the car.

"That's Daddy's coat," Jimmy said, glaring at me as we went down the walk. "Why is *she* wearing it?" Jimmy never spoke directly to me, but always addressed me through his mother. I wasn't sure if he did this with everyone, or if it was only me.

Jimmy was clutching a tambourine and Carol had finger cymbals. "They love to bring their instruments in the car, and that way we can sing while we drive. Right, kids?" Marty explained.

She buckled them into their car seats and they all began singing and banging out a kind of heavy metal version of Knick Knack Paddy Whack. I began to think that a simple beheading was too good for Justin.

"I guess you heard about the drowning? Such a shame," Marty said.

"So sad. Did you know her?" I asked.

"I didn't, but my friend Jan Dietz knew her. Jan knows everyone. I swear there isn't a soul in this county she doesn't know. Anyway, Jan says she was as nice as she could be. A lovely woman. Very quiet and unassuming."

"Yes, she was," I agreed.

"You knew her too?"

"I only met her once. She was going to take my class at the Art Center, and she showed me some of her work. She was very talented."

"What a waste. I'd love to know what she was doing all alone out in that row boat in the Choptank River at night. That just makes no sense," Marty said with a perplexed frown.

"They know it was at night, do they?" I asked.

"Apparently she shared a dock with a neighbor who said the boat was there when she went to bed that night and gone the next morning. The neighbor thought Louisa had lent the boat to someone, because she was going away. She has family in Maine. Often went up to visit for a week or so."

Marty pulled up in front of the school. "Want me to wait, Sarah, honey? Or should I swing back and pick you up after I drop the kids?"

"Why don't you drop the kids? Do you mind coming back for me?"

"Not the teensiest bit, sugar. I'll be back in a jiffy, and I'll wait right here for you."

"Thanks, Marty. You're a lifesaver."

I marched into school.

"Hello, Mrs. Landing. Can I help you?" Mrs. Jenkins, the receptionist, peered at me over the rim of her reading glasses, but I knew Justin would be in his Spanish classroom, so, rather than stop, I marched on relentlessly. Students and teachers leapt out of the way when they saw me coming, and Mrs. Jenkins followed, shouting, "You haven't signed in, Mrs. Landing."

I stopped outside the partially opened door of Justin's classroom. When he saw me his mouth dropped open and

45

the blood drained from his face. "M-M-Mom?" Quickly he
raised his hand.

"Yes, Justin?" his teacher said.

"Umm, may I be excused? My M-Mom." He pointed at
me, and the teacher nodded.

Justin came out into the hall and shut the door behind
him.

"H-hi, Mom. Is- is something wrong?"

"Yes, Justin. Something is wrong. Something is very
wrong. Would you like to see what I'm wearing under this
trench coat?"

"NO! Mom? Are you okay?"

"No, I'm not okay. You see, Justin, I'm wearing my
bathrobe. Do you think I usually go out wearing my
bathrobe?

"N-n-no, Mom."

"That's right, Justin. I only wear my bathrobe when I
can't get to my other clothes because I'm locked out of the
house, in spite of the four keys I have hidden in case of
emergency."

"I- I- I-" Justin's Adam's apple jitterbugged in his
throat. His eyes got huge and round. "I forgot, Mom. I kept
forgetting. I've been meaning to put them back, but every
night I forgot. I'm sorry, Mom. I'm really, really, really
sorry."

"We'll discuss it later, Justin. Just get me the keys." He
dashed back into the classroom and returned a moment
later with four keys. "I should keep mine, right, Mom?"

"Yes, Justin, you may continue to live at home, at least
for the time being."

It was now five of nine. I rushed down the hall and
back out to where Marty was waiting. If I hurried I could
still make it on time for the meeting with Brace.

At home I showered quickly and dressed in my good
suit and my one decent pair of heels. It was twenty of ten
when I rushed out of the house.

Ordinarily, twenty minutes would be plenty of time to
make it to Mr. Brace's office, provided there were no
unforeseen delays, but unforeseen delays there were. In
fact, if I were one to believe in conspiracy theories, I would
believe that there was a conspiracy to make me late that

day. I was dashing out of the house to the car, when, to my horror, I saw Mr. Hurd, our ultra-loquacious mailman coming up the walk, waving a registered mail envelope at me.

"Hi, Mr. Hurd. Just leave everything in the mailbox. I'm in a terrible hurry."

"That's fine, but you got to sign for this one." He stepped in front of me, blocking my escape.

"Okay. I'll sign."

I jogged in place, while Mr. Hurd took his time swinging his bag down, flipping through it to get the rest of my mail, and then pulling out his clipboard and pen. This was to be a lengthy procedure.

"It's terrible the way they make folks sign for everything nowadays, isn't it?" he said.

"It is," I agreed, making a grab for the clipboard. He pulled it artfully away and went on writing and making x's.

"Got to sign your life away when you get one of these," he said.

"Apparently."

"Usually not good news either."

"Usually not. Where do I sign, Mr. Hurd?" Finally I managed to wrench the clipboard from his hands and scrawl my signature in the three places he had marked. A registered letter, from a creditor, no doubt. Oh well. I already had stacks of them. One more was not going to change anything.

I took my mail and sprinted to the car, peeling out in a cloud of dust. For the next few minutes I sped towards town, and all was well until I found myself stuck behind a school bus that was stopping every other block. I sped down a side road, hoping to get away from the bus, but the road turned out to be a very narrow dead end. There was no place to turn around. I stepped out to survey the situation and sank up to my ankles in mud. Attempting to extract myself from the mud that was threatening to swallow me up like a pool of quicksand, I grabbed hold of a nearby bush and tore my new green blouse on its brambles.

Finally I managed to turn the car around and I proceeded to town. I could still make it on time if I hurried.

47

Naturally, the only place to park was miles away. I jumped out of the car and began to sprint. All was well until my heel broke, and I was propelled forward as if shot from a cannon. I landed on all fours, scraped a knee and cut my hand. Undaunted, I picked myself up and marched onward, until finally I arrived at Mr. Brace's office. I was limping. I was muddy and bloody. I had a torn blouse, a skirt that was streaked with dirt, a broken heel and torn panty hose, but I was on time. Triumphantly, I entered the building.

"I'm Sarah Landing," I said to the reception, who, crowned with a head set, sat queen-like behind a huge desk. She typed on her computer keyboard and pushed buttons importantly before turning her imperial gaze on me. She looked me up and down, and pursed her lips in disapproval, which was understandable, given my condition.

"You didn't receive the message, Mrs. Landing?"

"The message?"

"I believe it was your daughter I spoke with. I asked her to pass the message on to you, but apparently she didn't give it to you?"

"No. No she didn't," I said, vowing that the minute Grace got home I would sever her limbs from her body and feed them to the neighbor's cat. I sighed. "What was the message?"

"Mr. Brace has been called out of town unexpectedly. His mother is ill," she said in a hushed voice. "He would like to reschedule your appointment for two weeks from today, if that's convenient?"

"Two weeks from today?" I pretended to make a mental review of my busy and important schedule. "Yes. I think that will be fine."

She nodded briskly. "Very good. We'll see you then."

"Thank you," I said, marshalling my dignity, and attempting to make a poised retreat- not easy in a broken heel.

When I reached the door she called, "Oh, Mrs. Landing?"

"Yes?"

"Mr. Brace suggested that you bring your payment check to that meeting. If you need the exact figure of what you, uh, owe, just give us a call." She smiled brightly, pleased at her own helpfulness.

"That shouldn't be a problem," I said, blithely, sending a silent prayer of thanks to God, and Daniel Hollister. I wished I had a scarf to fling over my shoulder, but I did manage to call a devil-may-care "Good day" over my shoulder as I hobbled out the door and down the hall.

The woods were freezing and dark and eerily quiet, but they afforded him a good view of the house. And he had gotten himself a new pair of binoculars. Pretty damn strong. Made for extreme bird watchers. Or extreme criminals. He was neither one. He was just a man trying to survive. Through the windows he could see them, moving to and fro in the warm golden lamplight. Like a family in a dollhouse. A family like the one he could have had, if Louisa had listened to him. And maybe he still could. Louisa was gone, but maybe it wasn't too late for him.

And the keystone cops finally managed to recover the body. Only took 'em two weeks. Jesus. Of course, to give them their due, they didn't even know she was missing. That worked out pretty well if he did say so himself. The only person who even seemed at all worried about her was the ditz. Always calling Lou's cell phone, leaving messages. Jesus. Good thing he had taken the cell phone with him.

He watched the woman as she let the dog in, then locked the door. But she had keys hidden all over the place. Did she actually think locking the doors and hiding keys was taking precautions?

You'd think after the break-in she would at least suspect something was up. And those cops. Jesus. They were the most pathetic excuse he'd ever seen. That was why he didn't worry too much. Between the ditz and the keystone cops he knew there wasn't much to fear. He just had to find out how much she knew. He didn't think she knew much. Didn't seem like the suspicious type. As soon as the coast was clear and he wrapped up the loose ends, he could get out of there. It was time to get out and forget it all. Make a new life. He still had some paintings. And the book would bring in some funds. There was nothing to worry about. No one would find out now. Sarah didn't know. He was pretty sure she didn't know. Still, he would keep his eye on her for a while longer. Just to make sure. And then he would say good bye to this place once and for all.

Chapter Seven

In class that night I gave my students a slide show, with slides from some of the most outstanding picture books. I liked to give them an idea of the range and variety, and the excellence of the illustration. Images from Maurice Sendak, Chris Van Allsburg, Barbara Cooney, Ezra Jack Keats, filled the screen, and I couldn't help but wonder if Louisa Myner's name might someday have taken its place among these great artists if she had lived.

At home, I read to Geordie and when I finished the chapter I saw that he was almost asleep. I kissed him lightly and tiptoed from the room, hoping his dreams would be good ones.

In my own room I sat for a moment on the window seat and looked out at the river. It was a cool clear night, with only a sliver of a moon. The trees on the shore were silver against the black water, like an old fashioned silver plate photograph. I was watching them sway gently in the light breeze when I saw something else, a shadowy figure moving along the shore. I leaned closer to the window and peered out. It wasn't Justin or Grace, I could see that at once, but who was it? Why would anyone be out there now? As I stood up, I heard Paddington barking, and I hurried downstairs to see what was going on.

Paddington was at the door, scratching and whining. I opened it and she raced out, barking loudly. I followed at a

51

distance, not wishing to run into whoever it was I had seen from the window. By the time I got down to the dock, she was sniffing around madly, but there was no sign of anyone.

"What is it, girl?" I asked. "Who was out here?"

Paddington glanced up at me and wagged her tail briefly, and then continued sniffing along the shore. I shivered suddenly and felt very vulnerable. Whoever had been here couldn't be far away now. Was he watching me? Was he hiding somewhere on the shore? "Come on, girl. Whoever it was is gone. Let's go in."

But Paddington didn't want to give up, and she continued sniffing along the shore.

Justin was in the kitchen when I came back in. "What's going on, Mom? What's up with Paddie?"

"Someone was down by the shore."

"Oh, yeah? Who?"

"I don't know. Whoever it was was gone by the time we got out there, but I saw him from my window."

"You sure, Mom?"

"Of course I'm sure, Jus. I saw him myself, and Paddington heard him. And smelled him too. She was sniffing like crazy. There was someone out there."

"If you say so, Mom."

"I just don't know who it was."

"Or where they went."

"No."

Justin shrugged. "Prob'ly just someone who got lost."

"Why would someone who was lost end up by our shore?"

"I don't know, Mom. But what's your explanation? You're the one who saw this, um, person."

He had a point.

"Well, I would think maybe I had imagined it if it weren't for Paddington. But she definitely knew someone had been there." I swept up the crumbs that Justin had left and put his plate in the sink. "I'm going to bed, hon. I'm exhausted. How's your homework coming?"

"Almost done." Justin's perennial reply to any inquiry about homework.

"Okay, finish up and get to bed. You have a game tomorrow, don't you?"

"Yuh. Against Broward. Those assholes."

"Justin."

"It's true, Mom. They almost put Shaney in the hospital."

"Well, you better get a good night's sleep so you'll be ready for them."

"We'll be ready. Believe it."

The autumn chill was still in the air the next day, but the storms were gone. The skies were clear, the sun bright, and the air crisp, as if someone had come along in the night and scrubbed the world until it shone. The colors were glorious. The reeds and needle rush along the shore were golden and the leaves red and orange and yellow, reflected in the blue water and blazing against the cerulean sky. Soon they would all have fallen and only the black and grey and white of winter would be left, but at the moment it was breathtaking.

I quit work a few minutes early and headed out for a walk with Paddington. We ended up down on the dock. I sat, leaning against a piling, watching the white caps in the middle of the cove, and the constant motion of the river as it renewed itself again and again and again. Paddington sat beside me, her nose in the salty breeze, sniffing delightedly.

We shared the dock with the Sweeneys, and on one side their little rowboat creaked and moaned, creaked and groaned, as it bobbed in the waves, and on the other side our sailboat dipped and swayed, its halyards clinking against the mast.

I closed my eyes and might even have dozed off, when I heard Paddington's tail thump, thumping against the weathered gray boards of the dock. I looked around to see Marty Sweeney coming across the lawn followed by Jimmy and Carol, wearing their life vests and fighting over a tackle box. When they spotted Paddington, the children raced ahead to fling themselves at her while Marty followed at her usual calm pace.

Jimmy greeted Paddington ecstatically, patting her, smoothing her fur, and shaking her paw. Then he regarded me with his usual suspicion. "Mom. Is she going to fith with us?"

"Mrs. Landing is certainly welcome to. Wouldn't that be fun?" Marty said. Jimmy slid his fishing rod away from me and said nothing.

"I'd love to fish with you, but I'm just about to walk down the lane to meet Geordie's bus," I said.

"Geordie can fish with us," Carol said.

Jimmy nodded. They loved Geordie. Grace babysat for them and in their eyes she was practically an adult. Justin was a celebrity- they had been to some of his soccer games- and they basked in the glow of his cool, but it was Geordie, a mere mortal, not so much older than themselves, who occasionally gave them old toys he no longer needed, who taught them how to pick up a jellyfish with his bare hands, and the proper way to hold a blue crab without getting pinched. Geordie was the one they really loved.

"Well, I'll tell him you're down here. I bet he'll come down," I said.

"Yippee!" yelled Jimmy, jumping up from Paddington and grabbing his rod. "I'm gonna catch a hooge fith."

Marty took his rod. "Now, just be still till I get the lines baited," she said.

He began a manic sort of bouncing while waiting for his fishing rod. "That's a good boy, Jimmy," Marty told him. Apparently bouncing in place was as close as he came to being still. "How's Geordie's arm doing?" she asked.

"It's healing," I told her.

She nodded. "They do that at his age." Marty hooked a worm on Carol's line and said, "Did you hear they did an autopsy on that poor woman Louisa Myner?"

"An autopsy? Why?"

"Apparently there were some questions. She was known to be somewhat unstable."

"They're thinking she…"

Marty nodded. "Suicide," she mouthed the word so the children wouldn't hear.

I couldn't believe Louisa Myner had killed herself. It made no sense. Of course, when did suicide ever make sense? But why would someone with such talent throw it away?

"How sad," I said. "By the way, you didn't happen to see anyone out here by the shore last night, did you? "

"Last night. No, hon, I didn't see a thing last night. By the time we get these two to bed, well, I'm so bushed I fall in to bed myself."

Marty turned back to the children. "Okay, then. Let's catch some fish." They threw their lines into the water. "And if we do," she went on, "I'm going to take some out to Greg Myner. Poor man. He's over in Louisa's cottage, sorting her things and cleaning it out. A terrible job."

"Greg Myner? Louisa was married?" I asked.

"Greg is her brother. From Maine. I met him at Jan Dietz's house. She had a little dinner. He seemed very cut up about it, poor man."

Jimmy shrieked that he had a fith, and I said, "Well, I'm going to meet Geordie's bus. Catch some big ones."

"Tell Geordie he can fish with us," Carol said.

"I will."

Paddington and I left the dock and walked across the lawn to the lane. The breeze was picking up and the leaves were swirling around us as they made their journey from tree branch to the ground. The falling leaves always made me sad, at least, since Tom had died, because he and I used to rake them together on Saturdays and the kids would try to help, but mainly raced around excitedly. Then we would burn them and cook hot dogs over the flames. It was illegal to burn leaves now, and I hardly got around to raking them at all. I nagged at the kids to do it, but we usually only managed a few sad little piles.

We got to the end of the lane just as the bus pulled to a stop. Geordie jumped off and raced to where we stood. He hugged me and then Paddington who wagged her tail and spun in ecstatic circles, as if Geordie's emergence from the bus was the most exciting thing she had ever witnessed.

I thought about Louisa a lot over the next few days. Could she really have killed herself? It was too horrible to imagine. And her poor brother. I decided I should pay him a condolence call and return the draft of Louisa's second manuscript to him.

Chapter Eight

The next morning I went to the Railway Market and bought some cheese and cold cuts and a loaf of fresh wheat bread to take to Louisa's brother, and then I stopped by the Arts Center to pick up the draft of the manuscript. I hurried into my office, went to the files and flipped to the one marked Student Work. Because it was so early in the semester it had been the only piece in there when I put it back after the first class. But now the file was empty. The manuscript was gone.

Could I have put it somewhere else? Had I moved it? I searched the other files, then I searched the office, but it was nowhere to be found. Finally I gave up and went back to my car without it.

I drove out to the little cottage Louisa had leased. Carrying my bag of food like an offering, I knocked on the door.

"Coming," a pleasant voice called, and in a minute a male version of Louisa opened the door and looked inquiringly at me. "Hello," he said. "What can I do for you?"

"Mr. Myner?"

"At your service."

"I'm Sarah Landing. I knew Louisa."

He stepped back. "Please. Come in. I just finished making some coffee. Would you like a cup?"

"That would be great," I said, following him down the narrow little hall and into a bright, sunny kitchen that looked out on the river.

I held out my bag. "I brought you some things from Railway. I'm...so sorry. It must have been such a shock."

He closed his eyes and shook his head. "It's such a loss. Such a great blithering hole in my life. There's just the two of us. Our parents are both dead. But a shock? Not really. The truth is, I've been afraid she'd do this for twenty years. Ever since the first time she tried it."

"She's tried to- to kill herself before?" I asked.

He nodded. "Four times. My sister had Bi-polar disorder."

"I...I didn't know."

"Most people down here don't know. She wanted a clean start. And she seemed so good. She loved it here. At least, I thought she did."

"She seemed very happy when I met her. I wanted to tell you about that. You see, she had signed up to take my class. I teach at the Arts Center. The Art of the Picture Book."

He nodded and refilled my coffee cup.

"She showed me a copy of a manuscript she had done. *Jesse's Secret.* Have you seen it?" I asked.

"No. She never mentioned it, and I haven't found anything like that."

"Oh, dear. I was hoping you would have found it. It's wonderful."

"You say it was a manuscript? What kind of manuscript?" he asked.

"A picture book manuscript. I was very impressed with both the story and the artwork. She was a very talented artist."

"Louisa?" He said, sounding surprised.

I nodded.

"And there's something else," I said. "She left a draft for another book with me. It wasn't finished, but it was going to be wonderful as well. She still had some work to do on it, but if she'd had the chance, I think it would have been every bit as good as *Jesse's Secret.*"

"Do you have it? Can I see it?" he asked eagerly.

"That's what I came to tell you. The manuscript has disappeared. I- I feel terrible about this, and I was hoping you would have found the originals. I just can't understand any of this."

He sighed, took a sip of his coffee. "She always wanted to paint. She went to MICA at one point. Maybe she finally found a way to begin. But if she had, she hadn't shown me anything," he said sadly.

"Maybe she would have if..."

"Maybe. She was a very private person, though."

"Yes. I got that impression," I said. "And you have no idea where the originals might be?" I asked.

He shook his head. "I can tell you they're not here in the house, though. I've been through everything."

"Is there any other place she might have stored them?" I asked.

He thought for a minute, then shook his head. "None that comes to mind. I'll think about it though. You said she was going to take your class?" he asked.

I nodded.

"Last time I talked to her, she said she was into something new. She sounded good. When they called me to tell me..." he just shook his head.

"Well, I just wanted to offer my condolences and tell you how sorry I am."

We exchanged contact information, and I left him sitting forlornly at the table, staring at the bag of food I had brought him.

I was teaching that evening, and I decided to go into the center early and try to catch up with Connie. The main office was still open when I got there, and Connie's assistant, Jo, was in the middle of one of her stories. Two volunteer workers, Kate and Maureen, were sitting at their desks, turned toward her, listening raptly.

"It's the truth, so help me God. His expression!" Here Jo paused and shivered, closing her eyes as if the memory alone was enough to unhinge her. "You've never seen anything like it."

"That poor man," Kate said.

"Tragic," Maureen agreed. Both of them shivered along with Jo.

Jo's stories were fascinating, but they required strenuous audience participation. Her listeners were expected to act as a sort of Greek chorus, cheering her on to a dramatic climax.

"Still telling stories, huh, Jo?" I said, smiling.

"Sarah, honey! Aren't you a sight for sore eyes?" She gave me her wide warm smile, and came over to me, placing a plump hand on each of my shoulders, she peered into my face as if she were a doctor and I her patient. I wouldn't have been surprised if she had whipped out a tongue depressor and told me to say aww. "You look exhausted. And you're as skinny as a rail. You need to take better care of yourself," she told me. Jo was only a few years older than me, but she always treated me like a wayward child.

"Nag, nag, nag," I said, in keeping with our usual routine.

"Well someone around here has to keep the rest of you in line. Especially you and your friend there," she tilted her towards Connie's office.

"She here?" I asked.

"Go on in. She's in there. Unless she snuck out through the window. Which wouldn't surprise me the way things have been going."

"One of those days, Jo?"

"Darlin, you don't know the half of it."

I peeked in the door and saw Connie hunched over her desk. "Oh. You're working?" I said. "I didn't know anyone did that anymore."

"Editing the newsletter," Connie groaned. "Have you ever tried to read a paragraph that's been written entirely in the passive voice?" she asked.

"Nope. Sounds like fun," I said, pulling out the one extra chair.

"Wouldn't you think that anyone who's managed to get a PHD could construct a sentence?" Connie grumbled.

"I'm not sure you even have to be able to read a sentence to get a PHD anymore," I said.

She put the newsletter aside. "So, how's the new book

is going?" Connie asked. She was treading softly I knew, because the last time she had asked this, about six months ago, I had burst into tears. Today though, I smiled, and told her about Daniel's visit and the advance.

"Well, halleluiah." She came out from around her desk and hugged me. "I've been worried about you, girl."

"Huh. I've been worried about me too," I told her. We talked for a while until it was time for me to teach.

"Well, I better get down to my classroom. Let's do something soon," I said.

"How about tomorrow? There's the opening at the Wyecliff Galley."

"That's tomorrow? I'm glad you mentioned it. I'd forgotten all about it."

"Ben's out of town. You can be my date. There'll be wine. It may come in a box, but one can't be choosy when it's free. And, of course, all the rubbery cheese cubes and stale crackers you can eat. Maybe even some veggies and dip."

"Who could turn down an offer like that?"

"I'll pick you up at seven."

When I got home that night after my class, dueling iPods, hooked up to their speakers systems, were blasting from Grace's and Justin's rooms, and the TV was on in the den where Geordie was watching all by himself.

"Hi, sweetie," I said, stroking his hair. "What's going on?"

"Nothin'," he said. "Grace and Justin had a fight."

"They did? What about?"

"I'm not allowed to tell you," he said.

"Ahh,"

"Justin said if I do I'll never talk again because I won't have a tongue."

"Well, in that case I guess you better not tell me. I certainly don't want you to lose your tongue."

"No."

"And they're both still alive, right?"

"I guess."

"No broken bones? No massive blood loss?"

"Nope."

"So. Just another night in Paradise, huh?"

"Huh?" Geordie was again absorbed in the TV, not really paying any attention to me.

"This show ends in ten minutes. Then into bed, okay," I said.

"Yup."

I went upstairs and knocked on Grace's door. "Hi, hon. Everything okay? "

"Yeah. Except Justin is a complete asshole."

"Gracie," I said. I went in and sat on her bed.

"I'm sorry, Mom, but it's true. I just wish he'd grow up and act like a human being once in awhile."

"All in good time, my sweet, all in good time."

"Whatever. Oh, by the way, someone named Sam Prior called. He said to call him if you get in before ten. "

I looked at my watch. Nine-twenty-five. Sam was an old friend. He had been at Georgetown with Tom and me, and still lived in DC, working as an art dealer, though he had a small weekend cottage in Oxford. "I better give him a call," I told Grace. "You okay?"

"I'll be better when this dumb paper is done."

"All right, love. Come in and give me a hug before you go to bed." I kissed her forehead and left her to her paper. I hesitated outside Justin's door, but it had an aura that said, "For god sakes leave me alone," so I passed it and went to my own bedroom where I picked up the phone and called Sam.

"Listen, Sarah. There's something I need to talk to you about. Are you going to the Wyecliffe Gallery opening tomorrow?" he asked.

"As a matter of fact, I am," I told him. "Connie just reminded me about it."

"Great. I'm coming down for it. I'll see you there."

I was about to ask him what he wanted to talk to me about when Geordie called that he was ready for reading. I told Sam I'd see him at the gallery and we hung up.

True to her word, Connie was outside honking at seven on the dot the following evening.

It was already crowded when we arrived at the gallery. "Good turnout," I said. "I bet Liza's pleased."

"Yeah. We better hit the bar before the wine is all gone," Connie said, leading the way through the crowd. "Oh, look. Bottles with real corks. This is our lucky day."

"The appetizers are great," said Doug Firth, a local artist I had known for years. He and Tom had been fishing together just a few days before the accident, and it had taken over a year for his eyes to stop welling up with tears every time he saw me. "Liza's gone all out tonight. Try some a these little pink gizmos. They're real good."

"Hi, Dougie. I was hoping you'd be here." He was a big teddy bear of a man, as comfortable as a soft flannel shirt. He put an arm around my shoulders and squeezed, then kissed my cheek. "Likewise, darlin'. I'm always hoping for a glimpse of my favorite author. How's the new book coming?"

"It's coming, finally," I said. "It's taken forever, but it's finally happening."

He gave me a sad smile and said, "You've had a lot on your plate, Sar. I'm not surprised it's taken a while to get back in the game." He took a gulp of his beer, finishing half the bottle in one pull. "How're the minnows?" he asked.

"Good. Not minnows anymore though. Justin is a six foot tube into which one pours food."

"Ha. That's my boy. Like father like son. For a skinny guy Tom could really shovel it in."

"What about you, Dougie? Are you showing tonight?"

"I've got a few hanging over there. Most of my new stuff is over in DC now."

"That's great. They selling well?"

"Not too bad. Keeps me in beer." Doug had been married for a short while several years ago, but his marriage had broken up because his wife said he never did anything besides paint, fish and drink beer, which was true as far as I could tell.

"Speaking of beer," Doug held up his empty bottle. "I'm gonna get me another. You want anything, Sar?"

"No thanks. I'm going to go check out the paintings. I'll see you later, Dougie."

"You bet, darlin.'"

I was looking at one of Doug's ship paintings when someone beside me said, "Sarah. There you are."

"Sam. How are you?" I asked, though I was slightly shocked by his appearance. He looked ten years older than the last time I'd seen him just a few months earlier.

We kissed lightly, and he said, "Not so good."

"What's up?" I asked.

"Let's get a refill and I'll explain." He took my glass and disappeared. A minute later he was back with two more drinks. "Let's go over there," he said, leading me to a quiet corner.

"You knew Louisa Myner, didn't you?" he asked.

"Yes. I knew her, but only slightly. She was going to take my class at the Arts Center."

He nodded. "She told me. She was very excited about it."

"She told you?" I said, surprised.

"Yes. We were...friends. Well, more than friends. I met Louisa last year on the Oxford ferry. We both had bikes, and I noticed she had a sketch pad in the basket of her bike. We struck up a conversation about art, and that was it. I asked her if I could buy her lunch. We went to the park in Oxford and spent all afternoon talking. After that we started going for bike rides together, and within a month we were seeing quite a bit of each other."

"I didn't know," I said.

"Not many people did," he said. "I travel a lot, and I'm only on the shore on weekends for the most part. I was going through a messy divorce, and Louisa, well, Louisa was a very private person. I think we both felt that our relationship was a private thing. Just between the two of us.

"When I was in Washington I usually called her at least once or twice during the week, and the third week in September I called several times but got no answer. I knew I would be away the following two weeks, and I had hoped to see her before I went. I drove down here during the week to say goodbye, but again there was no sign of her."

He shook his head sadly. "I went away, and when I got back a week ago I heard that Louisa had killed herself. Well, I was devastated, of course. I still am. But I'm also shocked. I can't believe it. She was happy. She was thrilled that you were going to help her. I just don't understand it."

"Does anyone ever understand something like this?" I asked.

He shrugged. "I guess not, but..."

"Did you see her manuscript?" I asked.

"I did," he smiled. "It was wonderful."

"Yes."

Why was he telling me all this I wondered, and as if he could read my mind he said, "I guess you're wondering why I'm telling you this?"

"Well, the thought had crossed my mind," I said.

"Louisa was scared of something or someone. There was something she wasn't telling anyone." he said. "I just wondered if she had said anything to you."

I shook my head. "Louisa was ill, Sam. It's possible that she was imagining things."

"I know. Bi-polar."

"She told you about it?"

He nodded. "But it was a long time ago. She was fine. And so happy about the book."

Liza came over wielding a bottle of wine. "Sarah! Sam. I'm so glad you both came."

"Great crowd," I said as she filled my glass with more wine.

"It is. I'm thrilled." She sailed off to fill more glasses, and Sam and I continued our conversation.

"Louisa did mention that she might have to write under a pseudonym," I told him. "And she asked me not to say anything about her book. But that's all. I only met her the one time."

"Sarah. Do you have a copy of Louisa's manuscript?" he asked.

"*Jesse's Secret?*"

He nodded.

"No. She showed it to me, but she took it with her. I suggested she send it to my editor. Do you know if she did?"

"I know she was planning to, but whether she did or not I don't know."

"She left a draft of her new manuscript with me," I told him. "I put it in the files in my office at the Art Center, and now it's missing. I can't find it, Sam."

He rubbed a hand over his face and stared at me in frustration. "Her brother doesn't know anything about her manuscripts. No one has seen them. No one has them. And you and I are the only people who know anything about them."

He took out a card and gave it to me. "I'm going up to Maine tomorrow. I want to see her grave. If you think of anything I should know, please call me, would you?"

"Of course, Sam."

"Her book should be published." He put his glass down, kissed my cheek and left.

Chapter Nine

The following morning was my rescheduled meeting with Donald Brace, and though I was still dreading it, I wasn't dreading it half as much as I had been before I had the check for the seven thousand dollars I owed him. I had the money! I actually had the money. I did a little jig around my bedroom and sent a prayer of thanks to Daniel Hollister. We would not be living in our Bronco, at least for the next few months. I dressed in what, for me, passed as my power outfit, a black pant suit, made sure I had my check and the paperwork, and set off for the bank.

I pulled into the bank parking lot right on time and was congratulating myself on my punctuality as I locked the car when I heard footsteps behind me. I turned to find Donald Brace, in running shorts and tee shirt, jogging merrily toward me.

"Hello, Donald," I said.

'Well, well," he panted, jogging in place. "Mrs. Landing, isn't it?"

"Yes," I said tersely. Why was he out here? Why wasn't he waiting for me in his office like a good banker?

"I'm just going to hop in the shower and I'll be right with you. Ask Mrs. Speare to get you a cup of coffee while you wait. I'll be with you in a jiff!" he said cheerily as he sprinted off.

The shower?

As I stood before her desk the regal Mrs. Speare observed me over the top of her reading glasses, giving me a look of revulsion, as if I were an unusually distasteful form of bacteria. "Ahh. Mrs. Landing."

"Yes. I have an appointment with Mr. Brace. Shall I leave my paper work with you?" I asked.

"Please," she said, taking them from me. "He'll be a few minutes. Have a seat,"

I sat, trying to exude an air of quiet dignity, and felt that I was achieving my goal, until she rose from behind her desk and marched toward me, a piece of paper pinched between her thumb and forefinger. "This is not part of the necessary paperwork," she said, handing me a picture that Geordie had drawn of his teacher labeled 'Mrs. Poopy Parker.'

"Oh dear. I'm sorry. I must have scooped it up when I-"

"No doubt."

I picked up a piece of literature discussing the bank's policy of treating all its customers as if they were family. Hmm. Maybe. If Cinderella and her ugly stepsisters were the family they had in mind.

Eventually Mr. Brace appeared, clean and shining and wearing a dark suit and a tie so hideous that it could only have been chosen by a blind person.

"Now then, Mrs. Landing. I'm sorry you had to wait. Come in, won't you?"

He motioned for me to follow him into his office. He stepped behind his desk, but before he could sit down I handed over the check triumphantly. Ha! I thought. You won't be taking away the roof over our heads quite yet. He took the check, examined it and a look of blissful relief spread over his face.

"Oh, wonderful! Marvelous! Thank you! Thank you so much!" he chorused, dancing out from behind his desk. I shrank back, afraid he was going to hug me, but he got hold of himself and merely laid his hand on my shoulder. "I'm so pleased. I, uh, I know you've had a difficult time of it. I've been very worried about your, ah, situation."

Maybe he didn't actually relish the idea of turning widows and children out on the street.

"You and me both, Donald."

67

"So things are, um, turning around?"

"Yes. Yes, I think they may be," I said.

We exchanged a few more pleasantries, and he waltzed me out of the office and waved me off as if I were really were a member of the family. Ah, what money can do, I thought.

In the next few days I concentrated on my own book, which I had decided to call Wellington Wizard. There seemed nothing more I could do for Louisa, but I thought that perhaps I would honor the inspiration she had given me by thanking her in print when Wellington Wizard came out.

I was almost finished the first draft when I got a call from Daniel Hollister.

"Thank you for the DVD and the books you sent Geordie," I told him. A few days after Daniel's visit when Geordie had broken his wrist, he had sent Geordie the newest Harry Potter DVD, and some Diana Wynne Jones books as a get well soon present. "He's decided you're the best editor I've ever had."

"A boy with excellent taste. How's his wrist?"

"Healing," I said.

"And you got the check? "

"I did. Thank you. The manuscript is coming quite well."

"Wonderful. I'm so happy to hear that, Sarah. "

We talked for a while longer and we were just about to hang up when Daniel said, "Oh, one more thing. That other manuscript you mentioned when we had lunch? The one by your friend? Didn't you say it was called *Jesse's Secret*? About a boy who befriends a wood carver."

"Right."

"Well, we got it. Giles Leonard sent it in himself. Thanks for encouraging him. It's terrific!"

"You- you have *Jesse's Secret*? You have the manuscript?"

"Yes. My reader found it in the slush pile. It was addressed to me, and since I've just started here, she thought it must be a solicited manuscript, so she showed it to me immediately. I can certainly see why you were so impressed. This Giles Leonard is something."

"Giles Leonard? Is that the agent?"

"Giles Leonard is the writer/artist."

"But...Louisa Myner was the artist of the manuscript I had."

"Louisa Myner?"

"Yes. Louisa was going to be taking my class, and she showed me her manuscript. She did the art and the story."

"How odd. Perhaps she used a pseudonym?"

"Maybe," I said. "Umm. Do you know when the manuscript was sent?"

"I don't have the date, but I can check if it's important."

"It may be. You see, Louisa is dead. They found her body two weeks ago. She had been dead at least a week before that."

"Dead?"

"I'm afraid so."

"Let me do some checking and I'll get back to you."

We hung up, and I considered, not for the first time, the possibility that I was going crazy.

They were doing an autopsy. That wasn't great, but it also wasn't the worst. It would have been too good to be true if they'd just let it go. Why would a 50- something woman decide to take a midnight row in a tiny pram on a windy night? Even the keystone cops would have to ask themselves that much. And with her history, well, suicide was the obvious answer.

And that editor liked the book. No surprise there. Looked like that would all go pretty smoothly. As long as Ms. Ditz kept her nose out of things. He'd heard she'd been asking questions. Talking to people around town about what Louisa was like, and all. He didn't like it, but he wasn't worried at this point. She'd forget all about it soon enough, and how would she ever prove anything. It was a pretty safe bet she'd never figure it out. But still. He didn't like it.

Chapter Ten

The next morning I got an e-mail from Daniel.

Hi Sarah,

Jesse's Secret was postmarked in New York City on Sept 25th.

I am coming to DC again next Wednesday to speak at a writers' conference. I would love to get together with you afterward if you would have any interest in meeting me for lunch in DC?

September 25? That was before Louisa had died. And it was post- marked from New York City. So maybe Giles Leonard was her agent and she had sent it to him before submitting it to Pinnacle? But why wasn't her name listed as author?

I remembered her saying she may have wanted to use a pseudonym. Was Giles Leonard her pseudonym? I needed to find out more.

I wrote him back that I would love to meet him for lunch in DC, and I would also like to hear his talk.

I worked until early afternoon and then headed to town to do some errands and stop at the Arts Center. It was October 20th, and the Shore was in its glory. A few more good strong winds, and the leaves would all be down, but now they were beautiful. As I drove past the fields of soy beans, late corn and winter wheat I wondered how long it would be before these fields like so many others became housing developments or shopping malls.

The Arts Center was bustling. Maureen and Kate were hanging a new show in the gallery, with Jo directing them as if she were a traffic cop. "More to the left. No! Too much. Now just a tad higher. There. That's perfect. Now, grab the next one."

Maureen gave me a "Why me," look and said, "Who made her boss of the world?"

"Jo? Bossy? Imagine that," I said.

Jo shook her plump finger at me. "You better be nice to me, girl. I'm doing classroom assignments for next session tomorrow."

"Uh oh. Guess I'll be in the basement again."

"Raise it up a tad. Now a little to the right."

I left them to it and went in to my office to catch up on a few things. An hour later I was on my way home to meet Geordie's bus when my cell phone rang. Justin's voice seeped through the receiver.

"Mom. Uh, you're not at home, are you?"

"I'm on my way home now, Jus."

"Oh. 'Cause today's our scrimmage with Broward. I thought you might want to come."

"To your scrimmage?"

"It's Broward, Mom."

"I know, honey, but I usually just come to the games." I did try to go to most of Justin's home games, but scrimmages seemed unnecessary.

"Because there's kind of a problem."

"A problem?"

"My cleats. They're at home.'

"Yes?"

"Mom. Coach will kill me if I don't have them for the game."

"Can't you borrow a pair, sweetie?"

"Mom. Borrow someone else's cleats? That's gross. Besides, no one has an extra pair, and they wouldn't fit right."

71

Well, that was true enough. Justin's feet were gigantic. His shoes look like those extra big shoes made for clowns. It amazed me that he could run without falling over them.

"Look, Mom, I know this is like totally my fault. I know it was incredibly stupid and pathetic of me to have forgotten them, but could you, maybe, bring them down to school? Mom, I'll mow the lawn every weekend for the rest of my life. I promise."

"You promised that when I brought your math book down."

Silence.

"What time do you need them?"

"Not till 4:30," he said.

I sighed. "Let me see what's up with Grace and Geordie."

"Thanks, Mom. You're the best."

"No promises, Jus."

Grace was just getting home when I pulled up. She agreed to watch Geordie when he got home, so I raced in the house, grabbed Justin's cleats from the back porch and ran back to the car. I thought about a parenting course I had taken once. The instructor had been big on letting the child suffer natural consequences. Parents weren't supposed to fix things for him by picking up after him, or bringing him things he forgot. The idea being that if Mom and Dad were constantly bailing them out they'd never learn for themselves.

Ha. Obviously whoever came up with that parenting plan never had teenagers. If he didn't have his cleats, he couldn't run as well. He could get cut from the team, go into a deep depression, start taking drugs, drop out of school, and become a mass murderer. But then, if I was always fixing things for him he would never learn that actions have consequences. He wouldn't bother learning to do things for himself. He would find as he got older that he didn't have the skills and resources to take care of himself. He could drop out of school, not get a job, become a mass murderer. Hmm. Doomed either way, but at least by delivering his cleats I could avoid a miserable evening at the dinner table.

As I pulled into the parking lot next to the fields I saw Justin walking down from the gym with a group of boys. He was wearing a pair of floppy high top sneakers, his head was down and there was a kind of dejected air about him that I could feel all the way across the field. But then he looked up and saw my car, and he perked up. He said something to his friends and sprinted towards my car.

"Mom. You brought my cleats?"

"No. I drove all the way out here to tell you I couldn't manage it. Of course I brought them. And you own me big time."

"I know I do, Mom. You're the best."

I handed the cleats to him through the window, and he leaned in and kissed me.

"Thanks, Mom. Wish me luck."

"I do, sweetie. Play well."

Then he was off again, sprinting back to the bench. He was such a strange combination of grace and clumsiness. Energy that seemed to turn on and off like a light switch. There were no in betweens with Justin. He was either full of manic energy, a whirling dervish of movement and talk, or silent, sullen, aimless as a jellyfish.

I parked the car and wandered up to the field. There were a handful of other parents in the bleachers, but no one I knew very well. I sat down on the left where I would get a good view of Justin. The game was about to begin, and I watched to see if Justin would be starting when someone behind me said, "You're Marty Sweeny's neighbor aren't you?"

"Yes," I said, turning to see a woman who looked vaguely familiar. "I'm Sarah Landing."

She moved down a few rows to sit beside me. "I'm Jan Dietz. I met you last summer at their cook out."

"Yes, sure, I remember you," I lied. I didn't have the slightest recollection of her. "Do you have a child on the team?" I asked.

"A nephew. My sister's away and her son Chase is staying with me. How about you?" she asked."

"My son Justin is a left wing," I said, nodding at Justin who had just made what I thought was a pretty decent pass.

"You write children's books, don't you? *A Dog's Life?* Isn't that one of yours?"

"That's right." This woman had some memory.

"My Amy just loved *A Dog's Life*. I think it was her very favorite book. I had to read it so many times I think I memorized it."

We talked and watched the game, and then she said, "Did Marty tell me that you knew Louisa Myner?"

"Well, I had met her. She was going to take my class at the Arts Center."

"That was just the saddest thing. She was my parents' tenant. They just thought the world of her."

"She seemed like a lovely woman," I said.

She shook her head. "Such a shame, a disease like that. Of course my parents knew she had been ill, but they thought she was better. She certainly never showed any signs of instability the whole time she was living in our cottage."

"She seemed fine the time I met her," I said.

"I just couldn't believe it when I heard she was dead. There was just no indication..." Justin's team scored and we stood up, cheering.

"Of course, my mom said a friend of hers who knew Louisa in DC said she was a bit unstable."

"Oh, yes?"

Jan nodded. "Slashed up a painting at an art gallery in Georgetown, apparently."

"Really? Do you know what gallery? A friend of mine owns a gallery there."

"It's The Red Shoes Gallery. I could never forget the name. I even remember the name of the artist whose painting she slashed. It was Giles Leonard."

I felt the blood drain from my face. "G- Giles Leonard?" I stammered.

"That's right. I remember because a friend of mine had seen some of his paintings in New York a few years before and really liked them."

Justin's team scored another goal, and once again we stood up to cheer. And then the game was over. "Nice talking to you. Say hi to Marty for me," Jan said as she went off to collect her nephew.

Justin would get a ride home with his teammate, so I went to congratulate him and then left. On the way home I pondered this new information. Louisa Myner had slashed up a Giles Leonard painting. Louisa's book had been submitted to Pinnacle in Giles Leonard's name. What it meant, I couldn't fathom.

That night after dinner I googled the name Giles Leonard. I found several articles about him and some of the galleries where his work had shown, and images of some of his paintings. Though most of them were postage size, and many were oil paintings, there were some watercolors over pen and ink, and those, from what I could tell, were eerily reminiscent of the work in *Jesse's Secret*. The subject matter was different, but the style was very distinctive. Brushstroke, color, and use of line were remarkably similar. And so unique. Either they were by the same artist, or one or the other had been influenced by the other in a very significant way.

The next day I tried to call Greg Myner to see if he knew anything about Giles Leonard, or if he was aware that Louisa's manuscript had been submitted under that name. If it was Louisa's pseudonym, there was a good chance he would recognize it. I tried the number at the cottage, but got no answer. I thought maybe he had gone back to Maine, and I tried the number he given me for his home there, but got no answer at that number either.

Then, by a stroke of luck, I ran into him that evening in town. I had stopped in St Michael's to pick up a few things, and as I was leaving the grocery store I heard someone call my name. I turned around, and there was Greg.

"How are you, Sarah?" he said.

"Greg! How's the packing up going?"

"Almost finished. Just wrapping up some loose ends" I nodded.

"I'm leaving tomorrow," he went on. "Heading back to Maine. It's lonely work, and I'm ready to be done with it."

"I'm sure you must be. I'm so glad I ran into you. I tried to call you this morning. There's something I need to ask you," I said.

"Hey. We're right across the street from my favorite watering hole. How about joining me for a drink?"

I looked at my watch. It was Friday evening. Geordie was spending the night with a friend, and Grace and Justin were both going out. I was temporarily free.

"Sure. That would be great," I told him. "Just let me get rid of these."

He waited while I put my groceries in the car, and then we went across the street to McGills. We found a booth along the wall, and Greg ordered scotch on the rocks, and I ordered a glass of Pinot Grigio.

"So. Want did you want to know?" he asked.

"Well, remember when I asked if you had found a picture book manuscript? The one that Louisa had shown me?"

"Yes, but I'm afraid it still hasn't turned up."

I explained about the manuscript at Pinnacle. "But it was submitted under the name Giles Leonard. Did Louisa ever mention an artist named Giles Leonard?"

Greg closed his eyes and let his head fall back against the back of the booth. He blew his breath out in a heavy sigh. "Giles Leonard. Oh yes. Louisa knew him very well. Too well, you might say."

"What do you mean?" I asked.

He didn't answer for a moment, but stared down into his scotch, twirling his glass slowly. He took a long sip, and put the glass down carefully. Finally he said, "Louisa met Giles about ten years ago when she was living in Washington DC. She fell in love with him. And when Louisa fell in love, well, she fell madly in love. She became obsessed with him. They were together three or four years, and then Giles realized how unstable Louisa was. He couldn't take her possessiveness. He moved to New York without her."

Greg shook his head, frowning, and took another long sip of his scotch. "But Louisa didn't get over him. She basically stalked him. She'd call him and leave weepy messages. She even went to New York and tried to see him. Her friends and I tried to introduce her to other people, tried to get her to get some help, but she wouldn't let go of him."

He sighed heavily. "When he had a show in DC a few years ago, she went to the gallery and slashed up one of

76

his paintings. I had to bail her out of that one. Giles was very nice about it. I think he loved her too, but he couldn't deal with her self-destructiveness.

"After she slashed his painting, she went home and slashed her wrists. That was the third time she tried to kill herself. The first two had been years earlier, once when she was seventeen, and once when she was in her early twenties."

I nodded. I could see the lines of pain etched into his face, and I felt bad for making him talk about it, but I had to know.

"It was soon after that that Giles moved to France. He comes back now and then, I've heard, but not very often. I don't know if the move had anything to do with Louisa or not."

"But I heard that she'd gotten therapy after that incident, and was doing much better," I said.

Greg drained his glass and signaled the bartender for another one. "Well, I thought that certainly," he went on thoughtfully. "And people who knew her here seemed convinced of it." He shrugged. "The human psyche is damned complex. I've spent a lot of my life trying figure Louisa out. Trying to anticipate her moods." His second drink came, and Greg smiled sadly. "We were twins, you know."

"I didn't know that," I told him.

He nodded. "Louisa was...god we had fun when we were kids." He stared off, and I could see he was lost in some distant past before the demons that plagued Louisa had gotten hold of her. "Our parents were killed in a plane crash when we were sixteen. She was never the same after that."

"But I still don't understand what she was doing with Giles Leonard's manuscript. Or how she got hold of it." I said.

"I know that Giles comes back to New York now and then. It's possible..." he paused, "maybe he and Louisa were back in touch. Maybe he showed it to her. Maybe she was doing him a favor by getting your opinion. After all, Giles is an artist, not a picture book writer. He might have wanted an expert opinion."

77

I nodded. I could see how desperately he wanted to believe this, so I let it go. And it was possible after all.

I finished my glass of wine and said, "I've got to get going, Greg. Will you be back anytime soon?"

"I doubt it, Sarah. Without Louisa here..."

"I understand. Keep in touch, though, will you?"

"I will. I will," he said.

I left the bar, and I was pretty sure that I would never see the man again.

Chapter Eleven

The following Monday I was at work in my office when Sam Prior called. "Can I come over?" he asked. "I've got something to show you."

"Now?" I asked. I had planned to work all day. My deadline was looming, and I was determined to meet it. But something in Sam's voice told me it was important.

"Or this afternoon, if that's more convenient," he said.

"Come over around 3:00. Bring a fishing rod. We'll sit on the dock." I had called Sam a few days earlier and told him about *Jesse's Secret* having turned up at Pinnacle under the name Giles Leonard, but I hadn't talked to him since I had seen Greg, and I wondered if Greg had told Sam what he had told me.

At 3:00 on the dot the doorbell rang. I ran downstairs to find Sam waiting on my doorstep with a large envelope in his hand.

"That doesn't look like a fishing rod," I said.

He stared at me blankly, clearly confused. "I said to bring your rod. Remember?"

"Oh, yeah. I forgot."

"That's okay. We've got extras. But first, show me what you found." I led him into the kitchen and sat him down at the table. He opened the envelope and pulled out a notebook. "I had forgotten all about this," he said, holding the notebook closed in front of him. "One day last winter

Louisa was spending the night with me, and she didn't have her sketch book. I had some calls to make, and she had gotten an idea for one of the last spreads in *Jesse's Secret* and wanted to sketch it out. I gave her this notebook. She made several sketches, and I remember watching her when I finished my calls. She was remarkable. So quick. She tore one of the sketches out to take home, and the others she left in the notebook. 'I'll leave this here, shall I,' she said. 'That way, if I forget my sketchbook again, it'll be here.'" He smiled sadly. "I remember how pleased I was when she said that. Louisa was, well, she was very independent. For her, that was a big commitment."

He pushed the notebook towards me. "Here. Take a look."

I opened it and saw the sketches. They were rough, done in charcoal pencil, but they were definitely the roughs for the last spread of *Jesse's Secret*.

Sam went on. "She put it in a drawer in the desk in my den. She used it a few other times, sketching ideas for her new picture book. I forgot all about it. Yesterday I was looking for something, and I came across it."

I turned the pages and saw sketches that looked like the spreads in the new work Louisa had shown me.

"You see? It proves the work is hers." he said.

I nodded slowly. I was more confused than ever. "Have you talked to Greg Myner recently?" I asked.

Sam shook his head. "I thought he went back to Maine."

"He did, but I saw him before he left. He told me some things about Louisa..."

Sam waved my words away like flies. "That she was bi-polar and all that. I know. I know. She told me about it herself. But she was fine, Sarah. I'm telling you, she was not a person who was about to commit suicide."

I knew Sam didn't want to believe she had killed herself. And, like Greg, he couldn't bear the thought that Louisa had stolen Giles Leonard's work. I didn't know what to think, or what to say.

"You do see how important this notebook is. Don't you?" he pleaded.

"I do," I said. What else could I say? But secretly I thought that there had to be some other explanation. Maybe Louisa had seen Giles's sketches and copied them. She did have some artistic training, so she might have been able to do that.

"But it still doesn't tell us who Giles Leonard is. Or what his connection to Louisa is, other than an ex-lover."

Sam looked up. "An ex-lover?"

I didn't know how much to say. Greg clearly didn't want that part of the story known. He had told me as much. And Sam would only be hurt by knowing that Louisa had still been obsessed with Giles, even when they had been together. "Well, Greg said something about that," I told him.

Should I tell him about the slashing of the painting? I knew it would only hurt him. I felt it would be best for Sam, for Greg, and for Louisa if we all let it go. But I could see that Sam was determined to find out the truth.

"One thing I wanted to ask you," I said. "Did Louisa ever tell you what made her write *Jesse's Secret?* What gave her the idea for a picture book?"

"What do you mean?"

"Well, the art is... quite sophisticated. I know she spent a few years studying art, but that was years ago. And she had apparently given up painting. At least, there doesn't seem to be any evidence to the contrary. Were there other paintings somewhere? Other drawings? I mean, it's unusual that she would have gone from rarely painting to that level of proficiency. And starting with a picture book, I mean, it just seems odd."

"Hmm. I never thought about it. She didn't talk much about her life. She did go to art school, of course, so she had training. But as to why she chose to do a picture book, I really don't know. Does there have to be a reason? Doesn't it just happen sometimes?"

"Oh, sure. Of course...but most people usually have some reason. I always ask my students why they want to take the course. Sometimes they're would be writers who think picture books are easy- a misguided notion if ever there was one. Sometimes they are parents or grandparents who want to do one for their family, or teachers or librarians who have fallen in love with the form. Sometimes they're people whose art tends toward the whimsical, as it did in my case."

He considered. "None of those reasons really seems to fit Louisa, do they?" he asked.

"Not on the surface."

"What about you?" he asked. "What made you want to do picture books?"

"With me it was my kids, and seeing how many great picture books there were, and what a great form it was. And, my art was, still is, very much on the whimsical side."

He nodded.

"In fact," I went on, "as far as actual painting goes, Louisa is far more talented than I am. My work isn't weighty enough for painting, I've always felt, but it's perfectly suited to picture books. Louisa's seems more suitable for paintings, somehow. Of course, that's not to say that I don't think *Jesse's Secret* is wonderful."

"Yes. I see what you mean. And Louisa talked about painting the way an artist does. She knew about it."

I nodded, but I wondered if that could have been explained by her obsession with Giles Leonard.

"What about in her house?" I asked. "Were there paintings hanging? Was there evidence that she was working on other things?"

Sam looked thoughtful. "I- I was in her house so rarely. It was so close to the main house, you know. And Louisa didn't like the idea of the Willets knowing she had someone staying over. I picked her up there occasionally, and once, shortly after I met her she invited me for dinner, but mostly we met in town, or she would come to my house and we would cook together there. I- I just have to look into this. I have to find Giles Leonard. I think if I can find him, I'll find out the truth."

Again I nodded. I understood, but I was afraid the truth would hurt more than he knew.

"Come on. I've got to walk down the lane to meet Geordie's bus. Then we'll go fishing. I'll lend you a rod if you want. It's a beautiful afternoon."

He stood, taking his envelop. "I think I'll get going, Sarah. I've got some calls to make. I'll keep you posted on what I find out."

"Yes. Please do, Sam."

"Thank you. And, thanks for caring about this. It means a lot to know there's someone else who does."

He was not liking this at all. That flamer Pryor was back in town and stirring up trouble like he always did. He was pretty sure Pryor was one of the ones that put all this nonsense into her head to begin with. Him and that shrink. Making her think that she needed recognition. That "an artist needs to own her work." What crap. If Louisa had wanted to "own her work" why didn't she own it back when it wasn't selling at all, and she was too scared to even show up at a gallery or talk to any agents? Why didn't she tell him she didn't like the situation back then? Because she loved it back then. She didn't have to do a thing. It was all him. He had done it all. Everything. And then, when he finally made it start selling, made it a success, she decided she wanted to own her work.

He didn't like this Pryor showing up. He didn't like it at all. And what the hell does he think he's doing? What business does he have with Sarah? Jesus, he couldn't believe it when he followed him and saw him heading out to Starling's Neck. He still didn't believe he was actually going to see the ditz, but when he turned onto their lane, he had to believe it. If only he could have kept following and seen what he was up to. But he couldn't risk it. Too close for comfort.

He had always hated that guy. Pryor had always been toying with Louisa, he could see that. That asshole didn't care about her, not really. And they tried to keep the whole thing so hush hush. What was that all about? The guy is bad news. Damn. He couldn't believe he was back here sniffing around. He would have to keep him in his sights. The ditz is one thing. She didn't worry him, not when it was her. But Pryor was going to put ideas in her head. Just like he had with Louisa.

83

The traffic was heavy as it often is getting into DC, but I had foreseen that and for once had left in plenty of time. Even so I arrived at the conference just in time to hear Daniel's talk. He had said not to bother to come to hear him talk, and just to meet him after for lunch, but I wanted to hear him. I slipped into the back of the room just as he was being introduced. He was speaking to a group of novice writers, most of whom had not published, and, if truth be told, probably only a small percentage of them ever would. He spoke about the things he looked for in a manuscript, the feeling he got in the pit of his stomach when he saw a really good piece by an unknown writer. Yes, I thought. I knew that feeling. It was the feeling I had gotten when I first saw Louisa Myner's work. How sad, I thought again.

As I listened I found myself liking him more and more.

When he was finished speaking he took questions, and then patiently spoke to the writers grouped around him who were desperate for contacts with editors. I waited until the huddle began to clear a bit and went up to him.

"Ahh. Here's one of our most talented writers. This is Sarah Landing. Probably some of you are familiar with her work?"

A few of them were, and apparently feeling that they had wrung all the information they could out of Daniel, they turned the inquisition on me. "How long have you been with Pinnacle? Has he always been your editor? How did you get your first book published?"

"It was a while ago," I said. "It was easier then, I think. I was lucky."

"Nonsense," Daniel said. "She was talented. Talented and persistent and hard working. And that's what it takes."

I couldn't help noticing that he said was rather than is.

"Keep working and you'll all get there," he told them. "And now," he took my elbow and steered me towards the door, "I'm afraid we really have to go. Enjoy the rest of the conference."

We finally managed to make our escape, and Daniel said, "I made reservations at a restaurant on Connecticut. It's not far. Do you mind a short walk?"

"Of course not." I said. "Your talk was wonderful. I could relate to so many things you said." God what an idiotic remark, I thought. Let's see how many other clichés I can come up with.

But he seemed genuinely pleased, and said, "Well, thanks. It's always hard to know where to draw the line between disclosing the harsh realities of the profession and giving them the encouragement and the information they need."

"I know. I have the same problem with my students. I want to encourage them, but sometimes I wonder if I'm doing them a disservice when I know that the odds of most of them getting published are so slim."

"Exactly. But I fall on the encouragement side, usually. Even if someone's work is not publishable now, who's to say it won't be at some time in the future if they persist and keep writing?"

"That's so true. Although it's an unusual attitude for an editor. Most of the ones I know are quite cynical about unpublished writers."

"That's one of the reasons I like to speak at these kinds of things. It helps me to remember that actual people wrote all those manuscripts that pour in over the transom."

I nodded. "I can see how it would be easy to get cynical when you're surrounded by stacks of unpublishables. Do most of them come from agents now?" I asked.

"It's about fifty-fifty. We still do find gems in the slush pile now and then. Maybe one in 200 or 300 ~~hundred~~. That's what makes it so tough. Someone has to slog through all that mud to find the diamond. It can be overwhelming." He turned a corner and said, "It's right down here a block."

"You have first readers don't you?" I asked.

"We do, thank god, and they manage to winnow it down significantly. But I tell them to show me anything that may have potential, so I look at about thirty or forty a month. I do a lot of reading nights and weekends. Oh, the glamorous life of an editor."

He stopped, checked a slip of paper and pointed to a small restaurant across the street. "There we are. Spanacopita. Hope you like Spanish."

85

"Love it," I said.

It was a cozy little place with colorful tapestries hanging on the stucco walls, and good spicy smells emanating from the kitchen.

After we ordered, he said, "How is Geordie? Is he back to playing soccer yet?"

"Not yet. Another week in the cast. He's doing fine though. He loved the package you sent. Thank you. That was way beyond the call of duty."

"My pleasure. Geordie's thank you note was well worth it," he said, smiling.

I laughed. The note had said, "Dear Mr. Hollister, Thank you for the books and movie. I love them. You are my favorite editor my mom has ever had. I hope you stay being her editor. Love, Geordie."

"Quite a distinction. I was very flattered."

"Don't let it go to your head. You're the only editor I've had who's sent him a package."

"Well, I have to echo his sentiment. I hope I stay being your editor, too." He raised his glass. "Here's to a long and productive partnership."

I raised my glass too. "I'll drink to that. " I said. Boy will I ever, I thought.

"And Wellington is coming along?" he asked.

I smiled. "It is. Right on schedule."

"Wonderful! That's excellent news."

We talked business while we ate a delicious lunch, and when we finished, Daniel paid the bill and we walked back to the hotel parking lot where I had left my car.

"So, you'll be coming to New York soon?" he said.

"Definitely. Give me two or three weeks," I said.

"Good. Let me know when. I'll clear my calendar and devote myself to you."

When we reached my car I put my hand out, and he took it, but also leaned in to give me a kiss on the cheek.

"I, uh, I'll be in touch," I said.

"Yes," he said, still holding my hand. He seemed to have forgotten to let go.

"Well, thanks again."

"Yes." Finally he let go, and I slid into my car, thinking how much I liked him. Geordie was right; he was my favorite editor I had ever had too. And I too hoped he would stay being my editor.

Chapter Twelve

The Red Shoes Gallery was in Georgetown. I decided I would pay a visit to the gallery to see if I could find out anything more about Giles Leonard and his connection to Louisa.

I parked a few blocks from the gallery and walked through Georgetown, window shopping as I went. It was crowded, as Georgetown always was these days, but nothing like it was on weekends. I remembered my student days at Georgetown University, where I had met Tom. He was an engineering major, I an art and English double major.

Georgetown in those days had been smaller, less crowded, and less expensive. It had been a wonderful place to be a student. I had loved it, but Tom had missed the Eastern Shore even then, and couldn't wait for me to see it.

I remembered the first time he had taken me there, how he was so nervous and so excited. I could see him stealing glances at me, checking to see my reaction as we drove over the Chesapeake Bay Bridge. I hadn't loved it at first. I had thought it pretty, in an understated way, but slow and sleepy. Too hot in summer and flat, gray and muddy in the winter. I had grown up in Philadelphia, and I had spent vacations on the Jersey shore, with its bustling beach towns, sandy beaches and rough and tumble ocean. It had taken a few years for me to come to love the Eastern Shore. An acquired taste, Tom's father had called it, and so it was.

I came to the gallery, peered inside, and then pulled open the heavy glass door and went in. It was a large gallery with several rooms, each devoted to a single artist. I pretended to be examining the work while I waited for the young woman behind a desk to end her phone call. When she finally hung up, she smiled up at me. "Hi. I'm Jemma. Can I help you?" she said brightly.

"Just looking," I said. "These are beautiful."

"Yes. Everyone loves Robert's stuff. He's very popular," she said in a voice that indicated that everybody did not include herself.

I nodded.

"Are you looking for anything in particular?" Jemma asked.

"Actually, I'm looking for information about an artist who showed here several years ago. Giles Leonard."

"Giles Leonard?" She bit her lip, thinking. "It sounds sort of familiar, but I can't place him. I don't think he's shown here recently." She hopped up and said, "Let me check the computer. If he's shown anytime in last ten years he'll be in here."

She clicked away while I studied Robert's paintings.

"Here we go. Leonard, Giles. He had a small show here about four years ago. Sold three paintings, and oh..." she paused, read some more, and then said, "No wonder he's never had another show here." She said nothing for a minute, reading the screen with a frown. "It looks like one of his paintings was slashed."

"A painting slashed?" I asked. So it was true, I thought.

She nodded, still looking at the screen and clicking the key board. "We usually keep publicity files on all our artists. Let's see if there's anything." She turned the computer screen so that I could read.

"Here's a bio," she said. "Want me to print it for you?"

"That would be great," I told her.

She printed out a short paragraph that didn't say much more than one I had already read on the web. Giles Leonard was an award winning painter blah blah blah. No picture. No details.

"So you weren't working here when he showed here?"

"No. I came three years ago. And this would have been about four years back."

"Is there anyone around who would have been here then?" I asked.

She squeezed her lips together, contemplating. "Well, let's see. Deb came after me. And Cyrus, he might have been here then. But, Cyrus isn't exactly a font of information. But you could always talk to Feenie."

"Feenie?"

"Feenie Macvey. The owner."

Now we were getting somewhere. "Great. Where would I find Feenie?" I asked.

"Well, if you want you can wait. Or come back. She should be back in about half an hour or so. She'll definitely be back by 3:30."

I looked at my watch. It was ten to three. I had arranged with Grace to be home when Geordie got home, in case I hit traffic on the bridge, but still, if I waited, I wouldn't leave DC until at least four. I would definitely hit rush hour. I wouldn't be home until six or six thirty, but, of course, I was going to wait. I had to talk to this Feenie and find out if she knew anything. Curiosity alone dictated that much.

"Okay. I'll go and do a spot of shopping and be back in half an hour or so," I said. "And thank you so much. You've been very helpful."

"My pleasure. I hope Feenie can help you."

I left the gallery and headed down M Street, pausing along the way to window shop. I passed a vintage shop that had a gauzy pale peach blouse in the window that I knew would look fantastic on Grace. On impulse I went in and, though it was way more expensive than I would normally spend on something like that, I bought it. It had been so long since I had been able to buy any treats for any of us, I just couldn't help myself. Then, having bought something for Grace, I had to buy something for Justin and Geordie. Luck was with me as on the very next block I found a carved wooden African sculpture that was said to ward off evil spirits. Geordie would love it. And for Justin I found a sharp brown and red canvas messenger bag to replace his tattered and totally uncool backpack. In a pleasant state of buyer's exhilaration I took my parcels to my car and hurried back to the gallery for my rendezvous with Feenie.

Feenie was behind the desk when I returned to the gallery. She had short, sculptured hair somewhere between plum and magenta, and wore a green silk tunic over black leggings and cowboy boots. I approached the desk and she looked up and smiled a lovely smile that lit up her face and reached far into her eyes.

Are you Feenie? "I asked.

"Sure am. What can I do for ya?" she said, her voice carrying a hint of Scottish accent.

"I'm looking for information about an artist your gallery represented about four years ago. Giles Leonard. Jemma said you might be able to help."

"Giles Leonard. Yes. I know the name. Let me check here." She too began hitting the computer key board.

"Jemma said something about one of his paintings being slashed," I prompted.

"Oh, yes. Oh, it was awful." She seemed about to launch into the whole story, but then she stopped herself and gave me a suspicious glance. "You're not some kind of insurance investigator are you? They sniffed around a lot back then, but in the end Leonard didn't press charges. It certainly wasn't our fault. It was all directed at him. Some skeleton in his closet. He didn't want it all raked up anymore than we did."

"No no. I'm just curious for – personal reasons."

"Well, in that case, I'll tell you what I can, but I'm afraid it's not all that much." She pointed to a chair near her desk. "Have a seat."

I did, and she began her story. "A few days after the show opened, a woman came in and asked to see Giles Leonard's work. We showed her the paintings, there were only three, and before we knew what she was going to do, she pulls out a knife and starts ripping into one.

"Of course we all screamed, and young Marcos, who's not here anymore but luckily was in that day, jumps over the counter and leaps at her. She dropped the knife and ran out of the gallery. He chased her but lost her. We called the police, and they came and said they would investigate, but you know, they had about as much interest in finding a painting slasher as a pencil thief. It was not top priority. We contacted Giles Leonard's agent, and he sent an insurance inspector. About a week later, a man named Greg Myner came in. He said his sister was responsible for the slashing. She was unstable and had since been committed to a loony bin. History of bi polar disorder, etc etc. He asked for Giles Leonard's information. We gave him the agent's name, which is all we had, and Mr. Myner said he would get in touch with Leonard and make amends." Feenie shrugged and widened her eyes. "That was the end of it as far as we were concerned."

I thanked her profusely and took my leave.

Driving home, I thought Feenie's story pretty much dovetailed with what Greg Myner had told me, and what I thought to be true. It was pretty obvious that, no matter what Sam Pryor believed, Louisa was seriously unstable. She'd had four suicide attempts and had slashed up a painting. And it appeared that she had plagiarized, or plain out stolen, Giles Leonard's book, and tried to pass it off as her own. No wonder she hadn't told Greg much about her picture book project. He would know immediately that it wasn't hers. Would probably recognize Giles's work. Would probably have had her committed again. Maybe that's what she had wanted, I thought. It had been a cry for help. As soon as someone recognized the work, they would see how off she was, and get help.

But what about Sam? He seemed so convinced that she was healthy, and that she was an artist. Maybe he was just seeing what he wanted to see, something we all do from time to time.

I thought of the kids waiting for me at home, of the presents I had in my back seat, the first things I had bought for them out of joy and a relative sense of well being since Tom had died. I would not dwell on the sad case of Louisa Myner, or worry about the fact that the person who had begun my own recovery was a fraud. It didn't really matter how it had come about. The fact was that it had, and I had Daniel's check for twenty thousand dollars to prove it.

It was 6:45 when I pulled into the drive. Dusk had settled, and the house looked invitingly warm and snug. I stepped out of the car and stretched, and then grabbed my parcels from the back seat. A sharp wind blew from the river, and I shivered, feeling winter in the air. Inside, the house was surprisingly quiet. Peace reigned, and the lasagna I had made before I left smelled heavenly. Amazingly, someone, Grace or Justin, had thought to put it in the oven.

"Hi everyone," I called.

Thunder on the stairs. "Mom. God. Can we eat? I'm starved." Justin.

From the den, Grace: "He's already devoured the entire loaf of garlic bread, Mom. He's such a glutton. It's disgusting."

"What'ja get, Mom?" Geordie, noticing my parcels.

"I got a present for each of you," I told them.

Geordie's eyes widened. "A present?"

Justin narrowed his eyes suspiciously. "Why?"

"Are you okay, Mom?" Grace peered at me as if she was about to take my temperature.

I laughed. "I'm fine. I'm allowed to buy presents now and then. I had a little extra time in DC, so..."

The three of them stood together in a row, staring at me as if they didn't know what to make of me. Had it been so long since they had heard me laugh, or seen me look happy?

"Can we see?" Geordie asked.

I handed them each a box. Grace looked at hers and then back at me. "Shimmer? You got this at Shimmer?"

"Yes, Grace. People my age *are* allowed to shop there."

"Cool, Mom," Justin said, pulling out the messenger bag and slinging it over his shoulder. "I thought you said they weren't practical."

I shrugged. "They aren't. But style must win out sometimes."

"Cool." Justin leaped up, slapped the ceiling, and deposited the bag on the stairs.

"Mom, I love it," Grace said, holding the blouse up. "It's gorgeous. I can't believe you went to Shimmer." She jumped up and hugged me. "Thanks."

"What's that, bro?" Justin asked Geordie who was struggling to free the sculpture from its box.

"I don't know yet," he said, sounding intrigued.

Geordie read from the little booklet attached to the sculpture. "'This is an authentic African wood sculpture, used by tribes in the West Zambian plains to ward off evil spirits. It is said to protect anyone who lives in its home.' This is awesome, Mom. It's authentic." Geordie said, reverentially.

Justin looked at it critically. "I gotta say, if I was an evil spirit, this guy would definitely scare the shitake out of me."

"I'm going to hang him on the wall above my bed. Okay, Mom?"

"I think that's the perfect place for him."

Grace disappeared for a minute and came back wearing her shirt. "Oh, it looks lovely, sweetie," I said.

"I know. I love it, Mom."

"I saw it in the window, and it just had your name on it. I had to have it."

Geordie scrutinized the blouse. "I don't see her name on it," he said.

We laughed. "It's just an expression, Geords. It means it's perfect for me. Just like your sculpture has your name on it and Justin's bag has his name on it," Grace explained. "I guess the shopping gods were with Mom today, huh?"

"I gotta eat. I'm starved." Justin was shoveling lasagna onto his plate. "But, anyway, Mom. I thought you were going to meet with that editor dude. Did that fall through or something?"

"No. I went to hear his talk, and then we had lunch. I did the shopping after that. That's why I was so late getting home."

"So the deal's still on? You're still getting the money?" Justin asked.

"Yes, Jus. I told you. It's all set. I got the advance. I gave the mortgage money to Mr. Brace. And my new book is moving along well. So you can all stop worrying."

"When do we get to see the book, Mom?" Grace asked.

I considered. I usually didn't like to show my work until it was pretty much finished, except to editors and agents. But in this case I decided I should make an exception. They seemed to not be fully convinced that my book existed, and I couldn't blame them. I had spent the past few years with false starts, pretending to be working, and hedging about showing them anything because there wasn't anything to show.

"After dinner," I said.

"Really?"

"Really. I haven't completely finished all the scenes, but the storyline is complete, and I have roughs of the whole thing, and most of the finals. You can see it."

"Whoa, Mom. You've been bookin' it," Justin said.

I nodded. "Once I got started with this one, it just came right along."

"Is it about that little guy with the wand and the cape?" Geordie asked. "I saw his picture on your easel."

"Yup."

"Good. I like him."

"I hope you'll like the whole story," I said.

"I will," Geordie said, attacking his lasagna.

We moved on to the subject of what assholes Broward's soccer team members were, and when Grace was going to take her driver's test.

We were almost finished dinner when Geordie asked, "What's his name, Mom?"

"Wellington. Wellington Wizard," I told him, knowing exactly who he meant.

"Wellington," Geordie said, his face serious, considering. He gave a quick nod of approval and said it again. "Wellington. It's a good name, Mom."

And when he smiled at me, I whispered thank you, not to Geordie, though he thought I was talking to him, but to whoever had arranged for Geordie to inherit Tom's smile, a smile that always managed to warm and comfort me as surely as a ray of sunlight on a winter morning.

Chapter Thirteen

A week passed. My deadline for *Wellington* was fast approaching, and I had been thinking of little else but my upcoming trip to New York, and my meetings with Daniel and Katharine. I was happy and felt that it was a bright, cheer June of the soul, rather than Melville's dark drear November, even though it was November, and a rainy dark and drear one at that. With the left over money from the advance, I had gotten the roof fixed, and the dish washer repaired. We were, for the time being, solvent. And my work was going great.

Daniel Hollister had taken to calling frequently, mostly to check on my progress and sometimes with small questions about my earlier work. He was trying to find other markets for them, book clubs and things, and I was immensely grateful for the help he was giving me. We always ended up talking for quite a while, and I found myself looking forward to his phone calls. In the last few years I had dreaded calls from my editor, knowing I was only going to disappoint her. But Daniel was different, and I was happy.

Then I got a message on my answering machine from Sam Pryor. "Sarah, look. I've got a lot to tell you. I know who Giles Leonard is. I'm coming down to the shore tomorrow. I can't talk now, but could you meet me at my house at four o'clock tomorrow afternoon? Please come. It's important or I wouldn't ask."

When I first heard the message I was irritated. I was done with this, wasn't I? I hadn't known Louisa that well, and, while I understood Sam's pain and felt for him, I was tired of grieving lovers and dark obsessions. I had been grieving too long myself, and now that it was spring again in my heart, I didn't want to be reminded of that dark place.

Not that I didn't miss Tom every day. And not that his memory wasn't as alive as it had always been. But I didn't feel like half a person anymore, and I wanted to savor my new whole self for a little while.

I tried to call Sam several times that evening and the following morning, but when I couldn't get him, I decided I would do as he asked and meet him at his house. I was going to have to tell him what I had found out about Louisa slashing up Giles Leonard's painting. I would tell him that it seemed to me that Louisa had been sick, and had somehow gotten Giles's picture book and pretended it was hers. I would tell him that he should accept her death as a suicide and move on.

As I drove out to Sam's cottage I rehearsed my speech. It was quite convincing, and if it didn't convince him, it would at least get him to leave me alone. I was almost to Sam's driveway when I saw a car pulling out of it. I slowed, and as the car passed me I saw that it was the man with the gray ponytail, the same man I had seen the time I went to Louisa Myner's house. I turned into Sam's driveway at a few minutes past four.

I got out and went to the door and knocked. No answer. I waited, knocked again. No answer. I looked around. Sam's car was not in the driveway. I sat down on the front steps waiting. After a few minutes I looked at my watch. It was a quarter past. I tried to call Sam on his cell phone but got his voice mail. I decided I would wait until 4: 30.

It was a lovely late afternoon, but quite chilly, and the pale November sun was already low in the sky. I stood up and walked around the house for a glimpse of the river, and on the path I saw something gleaming in the sun. I stooped for a closer look and saw that it was a silver pen. I

picked it up and found that it was a Mark Cross Pen- quite
nice- and was engraved with the initials GL. I was
suddenly quite certain that the initials stood for Giles
Leonard, and that the gray pony tailed man was none other
than Giles Leonard himself. Sam said he had figured out
who Giles Leonard was. Probably he had asked him to
come here to meet with us. When Sam hadn't been home,
Giles had probably waited a few minutes and then left.

I waited a few more minutes, tried to call Sam again,
and finally gave up in frustration and went home, feeling
certain that Sam would call soon and explain what had
happened and why he had missed our meeting. Traffic on
the bridge, probably. But why hadn't he called? Why hadn't
he answered my calls? I was beginning to think Sam was
as crazy as Louisa Myner.

Everyone was home when I got there, and everyone
needed me for something.

Grace met me at the door waving a calendar in my face,
"Mom, I have to get my driver's license by next Saturday?
When can you take me?"

"Possibly this Saturday, but are you sure you're ready?"

"Ready? I've been ready for two years."

"But, I mean, are you sure you can pass?"

"Of course. If Tracy Gains can pass, I can pass."

"Tracy Gains has a license?" Justin asked.

Grace nodded. "She got it yesterday."

"Jesus, that's scary," Justin said. "Some people just
should not be allowed to drive."

"I think I can take you Saturday, but why do you need
it by next weekend?"

"A bunch of us want to go to Ocean City for the day."

"And you plan to drive a carload of kids there the first
week you have your license? I don't think so," I said.

"Told ya," Justin smirked.

In fact, I had just read a memo from the school that
said their policy for student drivers was that until kids had
had their license for six months they could only drive with
one other student in the car, and suggesting that parents
follow the same rule. I'm sure Grace was hoping I had
missed that memo, which was often the case, but this time
I foiled her.

"We'll be following the school policy. One rider until you've been driving for six months. Besides, I'll need the car."

She looked at me defiantly. "I'll take Dad's truck," she said. "I mean, it's about time someone used it."

Justin and Geordie stared at her as if she had just stepped out of the phone booth wearing a superwoman outfit.

Justin swallowed. He did his bobble head routine, Adam's apple working overtime. "It is, Mom. It's time," he mumbled.

Geordie nodded solemnly. "It's bad for trucks not to be drived, Mom." He spoke gently, as I were a small child who might not understand.

The subject of Tom's truck was one that everyone, including my sister, the kids, our friends, even our neighbor Skip Sweeney had tried and failed to engage me on. The truck sat in its place in the garage, the place where Tom had parked it every night, and it had moved exactly twice in the three years he'd been dead.

The first time was about six months after Tom's death, when my car had gone to the shop. I had loaded everyone into the truck to drive them to school, backed it out of the garage, stopped in the middle of the driveway, turned it off, climbed out, and, with tears streaming down my face, ran into the house and up to my bedroom where I cried for half an hour while the kids sat on the front steps waiting. Finally, Grace had called Connie, and Connie had come over and put the truck back in the garage. Then she came upstairs and helped me pull myself together. When we came downstairs Connie told the kids, "I'll drive you guys to school and then your mom and me will go get a loaner. She's just not ready for the truck yet."

The second time was when Dougie Firth asked me if he could borrow the truck to move some furniture. I believe this may have been a conspiracy between him and Connie and the kids. I said sure, glad to have Dougie use it, but when he brought it back and I caught sight of it bouncing down the lane, I thought for just a split second that it was Tom, and again, the tears flowed, and I retreated to my bedroom.

99

That had been almost two years ago, and no one had mentioned the truck since. It sat in its space in the garage, like an elephant in the living room that everyone pretends not to notice.

But the kids were right. It was time. I looked at them and nodded. "Yes. We'll need it now that you'll be driving, Gracey," I said calmly, as if the only reason we hadn't used it lately was because we didn't need to. "We'll get it into the shop, and get it tuned up."

And that was it. We ordered pizza for dinner. Justin proceeded to explain to us in gory detail the depths of depravity to which the Broward team and everyone associated with Broward had descended, and Geordie recited his lines-um, line- for the Thanksgiving play in which he portrayed a Native American introducing corn (maize) to the Pilgrims. It seems there are many, many ways in which one can say, "Maize good. Try. You will like." We were treated to approximately 200 renditions that evening. And so it was that Sam Pryor and his quest slipped my mind.

He'd been listening to Sarah's messages on her answering machine for a few weeks now. Figuring out her pin number was the work of five minutes- of course. Mostly ditzy friends who sounded just like her, or that editor, Hollister who called her every five minutes. Their editor, he should say. Wonder if he'd call him that often. Somehow he doubted it.

But Hollister had been causing some problems too. He'd been emailing him, wanted some changes to the book. Changes were not about to happen. If Hollister liked it so much, he could take it as is. And that's what he had told him. What was he supposed to do? Come back from the South of France just to meet with a picture book editor. Not gonna happen.

Anyway, there hadn't been anything too disturbing on Sarah's phone until the call from Pryor. I know who Giles Leonard is, Pryor had told her. He seriously doubted that Pryor did know, but he couldn't take any chances. He decided a trip to DC was in order. He would go tonight. He had to go before Pryor met with Sarah, because if he really did know...well, he wouldn't be meeting with her. And if Pryor didn't know, well, it would all work out very nicely. He might be able to get this so-called proof Pryor had. And then he would see what happened.

Chapter Fourteen

I did try to call Sam again, but after several more times not getting him on his cell phone, I decided I had his number wrong, and I figured he'd call me when he was able to. The next day I went back to work on my book, and it wasn't until I went into the Arts Center that afternoon that I found out that Sam Pryor was dead.

It was Jo who told me. I had just walked in the door, and she was sitting at her desk. "Hello," I said, cheerfully.

Jo looked up. "You haven't heard." It wasn't a question. She knew by my cheery demeanor that I hadn't heard.

"Haven't heard what? Has the mayor slashed our budget again?" I asked. But one look at Jo's face told me it was much worse than that.

"It- It's Sam Pryor."

"Sam? He's here? I was supposed to meet him yesterday afternoon but-"

"No, No. He's not here, Sarah. He's d- dead."

"What?" I dropped my bag and slumped into the chair beside Jo's desk.

Jo nodded. Terry Malone just called. His house in DC burned to the ground two nights ago. Sam was inside."

"I -I was supposed to meet him out at his place at four yesterday afternoon, but he didn't show up. I've been trying to call him..."

I looked at Jo. Her eyes were red rimmed as if she'd been crying, and her usually cheerful face was pale. She had known Sam as long as I had, longer probably. She shook her head. "I just can't believe it," she said quietly.

"Do they know what caused it?" I asked.

He had a studio on the top floor of his house. He was an amateur painter. A lamp was tipped over and caught some combustible rags on fire.

"Wasn't there a smoke alarm? Didn't he wake up?"

"The smoke alarm malfunctioned- dead battery. And he had a prescription for sleep medication..." Jo shrugged.

I looked at the closed door behind Jo. "Does Connie know?" I asked.

Jo nodded. "But she's at a meeting in Annapolis. She said to tell you she'll call you later."

I sat there for a few more minutes, feeling stunned. "First Louisa. Now Sam," I said. "Did you know they'd been seeing each other? Before she died?"

"Louisa?" Jo asked.

"Louisa Myner. The woman who drowned back in September."

"I thought she killed herself," Jo said.

"That's what the police thought. But Sam never believed it."

"They'd been dating? She and Sam?" Jo asked.

I nodded.

"I didn't know that. I didn't know her. She hadn't been here long, had she?"

"Just a few years. She was signed up to take my class. It's odd, isn't it?" I asked.

"What do you mean?" Jo said.

"I mean, here they are, the two of them, both dead. And Sam was convinced that Louisa did *not* kill herself."

"So, he thinks- thought- she was...murdered?"

"No. Yes, I guess. I don't know what he thought, Jo. And now we'll never know." I stood up. "Tell Connie to call me as soon as she gets back. I've got to go see someone."

I had to talk to Dougie Firth. He knew Sam well, and he might know something about Louisa. I called him on my cell phone.

"Dougie, it's Sarah."

"Hi, babe. You heard, huh?"

"Yeah. I can't believe it, Dougie."

"Me neither. I just saw him last weekend. We went fishing."

"Look, Dougie. I need to talk to you. Can I meet you somewhere?"

"Sure, Sar. I'm in the studio. I'll meet you in McGill's in what, half an hour?"

"Great. See you then," I said.

When I stepped into the dark interior of McGills's it took a moment for my eyes to adjust. When they did, I saw Dougie sitting in a booth near the back, reading the *Star Democrat*. He waved, and I headed for him. He stood up and wrapped me in the bear hug that was one of the things that had helped me get through Tom's death. There was something infinitely comforting about Dougie.

"How ya doing, Sar?" he asked.

"I'm okay, Dougie. I was great until I heard about Sam. Work's going well, finally, and the kids are doing alright."

Dougie nodded. "That's good. New book comin' along?"

I nodded. The waitress appeared and Dougie ordered another beer. "I'll have an ice tea. Unsweetened, please." I told her.

"So what can I do for you, Sar?" he asked.

"I just need to find out some things, Dougie. You knew Sam pretty well, didn't you?"

"Well, I knew him for a long time. Since we were kids. But I don't know if anyone knew Sam well. Know what I mean?"

I nodded. I did know what he meant. Sam, like Louisa, was a private person. Not easily known at all.

"Did you know he was seeing Louisa Myner?"

"Seeing as in a relationship?"

"Yes. They met about a year ago, and had grown quite close from what he told me. Sam didn't believe that Louisa killed herself."

"He thought it was an accident?"

I shrugged.

"Why would she go out in a little row boat with no lights in the middle of the night unless she wanted to kill herself? It doesn't make any sense."

104

"I know. That's what he said. He said Louisa would never have done such a thing."

"But what did he think happened then?" he asked.

"I think he suspected foul play."

"Foul play? You mean, murder?"

I nodded.

"But who? Why?"

"That's the million dollar question. Or two questions."

"What made him think that?" Dougie asked.

"Have you ever heard of an artist named Giles Leonard?"

"Giles Leonard? Sounds vaguely familiar. Where's he located?"

"He used to live in New York, but now I hear he lives mostly in France. He used to show regularly in New York, and occasionally in DC, but he hasn't shown much in the last five years, and no one seems to have seen him in even longer."

"Like I said, the name sounds familiar. I might have run in to him back in the day." He took a long sip of his beer. "So, why the interest?"

I told him about *Jesse's Secret*, but I left out some bits. I didn't tell about the slashed up painting, or about the notebook. He listened attentively, his chin cupped in his hand, occasionally sipping his beer meditatively. When I finished he frowned and shook his head slowly. "That is a very strange tale."

"I know. I don't know what to make of it."

"And now both Louisa and Sam are dead," he said sadly.

I nodded.

Dougie sat back thinking. "Has Louisa ever painted, that you know of? Besides the paintings for the books?"

"I don't think so. Though she did go to art school at one time, so I've heard."

"And her work looks very similar to the things you've seen of Giles Leonard?"

"Yes. There were some things on the web. That type of thing. I haven't actually seen any of his paintings hanging. As I said, he hasn't shown in a while and hasn't been around much for quite a while."

"You want me to call some people I know in New York? See if I can find out anything about this Giles Leonard?"

"Would you, Dougie?" I was glad he had offered before I asked. I wasn't sure how I would explain my interest, except that Sam was a friend, and …well, as he said, something fishy was going on.

Chapter Fifteen

Three days later I was on the train on my way to New York City, with a completed rough draft of *Wellington's Wand* in my briefcase. I hadn't been to New York in over a year, and I was excited. I was having lunch with Daniel and dinner with Katharine Briggs, my agent. Katharine had seen none of *Wellington,* and I couldn't wait to show it to her.

As the late autumn landscape flew by, I thought of *Jesse's Secret* and wondered what was happening with it. I thought about the notebook that Sam Pryor had shown me. There was the same haunting quality about the drawings in the notebook that I had seen in *Jesse's Secret.* They were impressionistic, but there was an edge to them, something inexpressible that hinted at the unknown, the other worldly. The same quality that made *Jesse's Secret* so compelling. I decided that if the right time came, I would tell Daniel everything I knew. I felt I knew him well enough now. And I trusted him. Maybe he could help me sort it all out.

Across from me a young woman talked loudly on her cell phone, and the man across the aisle rattled his paper and looked at her with annoyance. She finally took the hint and lowered her voice slightly but went on talking and laughing. I must have dozed off because it seemed only a few minutes later I heard the announcement for Penn Station.

I dropped my bags at my hotel and caught a cab to Pinnacle.

I gave the receptionist my name, and in a minute I saw Daniel coming down the hall to greet me, his smile warm and his eyes bright. He took both my hands in his and kissed me lightly on the cheek. "Well! The day we've all been waiting for. We finally get Ms. Landing to New York."

"Yes. The country mouse comes to the big city. I hope I managed to get the hay seeds out of my hair."

He made a show of inspecting my hair. "I see no signs of hay seed. In fact," he paused and glanced surreptitiously at my dress, "if I didn't know better I'd swear you were a native. One who eats poor editors like me for lunch."

He introduced me to the receptionist- there seemed to be a new one each time I came- and steered me down the hall to his office.

"How was your trip?" he asked.

"Great. I love trains. They seem so, I don't know, full of possibilities."

"Hmm. The ones I'm on are usually just full of annoying people shouting into cell phones."

"That too," I said, smiling.

He had a corner office with a great view of midtown Manhattan. Besides his desk and bookshelves, there was a small conference table, and in one corner a little fridge with a coffee maker on top.

"Wow. Not bad. What did you do to rate this space?" I asked.

"It was quite simple, really. I lay on the floor and refused to move until they let me have it. Bit uncomfortable by the third day, but well worth it in the end."

I laughed, and he pulled out a chair at the conference table. "Have a seat. Would you like tea or coffee? A bottle of water?"

"Oh, no thanks, I'm fine.

He brought a pen and note pad and joined me at the table. "So. You've made some progress?"

I nodded, opened my brief case and took out the folder that contained my draft. "I have, but it's still rough," I said, offering him the folder.

"Of course." He took the folder, and plucked a picture book off the bookshelf and handed it to me. "This is a review copy of Morris Van Meter's latest. Have a look while I glance through this."

I loved Morris Van Meter's work, and normally I would be thrilled to get a sneak preview of his new book, but of course I only wanted to see Daniel's reaction to my own book. I pretended to be absorbed in *Carnival Night*, but surreptitiously I watched his face as he turned my pages, studying each one slowly, seriously, his face betraying nothing of what he might be feeling.

When he was finished he closed the book, squared it in front of him, and folded his hands. I had decided he hated it when he cleared his throat and looked up at me. I saw that my book had affected him deeply, and he was trying to compose himself.

"It's...exquisite."

"You like it?"

He laughed. "Like it? I adore it. It's funny, it's charming, it's moving..." He shook his head and shrugged. "It's everything a picture book should be."

"I'm so pleased," I said, though I was way more than pleased. I was so happy I had to hold on to my chair to keep myself from leaping onto the conference table and dancing a jig. I had hoped he would like it. I had even dared to hope he would love it. But his reaction had been more positive than I could have imagined, and I was thrilled.

"You should be pleased," he said. "Pleased with yourself for creating such a terrific book. Now, we need to go over some things. First of all, let's get a time line in place that will ensure we get it into the spring list. Do you have your calendar?"

I took out my calendar and we talked about timing, and then moved on to some of the other details that went into the editing and publishing process.

It was past one o'clock when he said, "Well, I don't know about you but I'm famished. Are you ready for lunch?"

"Absolutely."

"Good. How do you feel about Armenian food? There's a place a few blocks from here that I've been meaning to try. It's supposed to be excellent."

"Sounds great. I have no clue what Armenian food is, but I'll take a chance. I like anything cooked by someone other than me. Especially if it doesn't come in a cardboard box."

"Ahh. I'm not really sure what Armenian food is like myself, but I'm pretty sure it will come on a plate, and I promise you won't have to cook. Or wash dishes."

"And I'm assuming the conversation will not center on whether Geordie can burp louder than Justin or whether or not Grace's math teacher is bipolar?"

"Definitely not, though I'm sure Ian would be happy to weigh in on the burp issue if they need an unbiased opinion."

I laughed, and as I stood up I noticed some photographs on the bookshelf. I stepped closer and saw a boy about ten, small, with a shock of dark curly hair, looking into the camera with an expression of amused affection, and Daniel's eyes.

"Speak of the devil," Daniel said.

"He's lovely. He has your eyes."

"And his mother's nose, fortunately."

I moved to the next frame, Ian with a man and woman and another boy, slightly older I guessed. They were standing on a hillside, laden with back packs and camping gear and looking anxious to get underway.

"Ian with my sister and her husband and their son Niles. We were hiking in the Cotswold's. Last summer."

"You're the photographer?"

"Yes. They were most annoyed with me for stopping constantly to take photos. Particularly Ian. He thinks it's a disgusting habit."

I noticed several other larger framed photographs, scenic shots of a full moon rising above a snow covered mountain, a group of sailboats silhouetted against a red sky, and a stormy sky over a meadow filled with autumn leaves in a swirling mass of color. "These are beautiful," I said. "Did you take them?"

"I did. Just lucky shots," he said, but I could tell he was pleased with them.

"Well, shall we?" he said, ushering me out the door.

The restaurant was a small bistro that glowed warmly with a wood fireplace, and smelled deliciously of garlic, and rich winey sauces.

"Mmm." I took a deep breath. "Heavenly."

"We shall soon discover what Armenian food is like," he said.

The hostess showed us to our table and gave Daniel a wine list. "Any preferences?" he asked.

"I usually drink white, but I'm happy with red too, if you'd rather."

He ordered a bottle of Pinot Grigio that was yummy, and when the waiter had poured our glasses and had taken our orders, Daniel raised his glass to mine. "To *Wellington's Wand*. May it live forever."

I clinked my glass with his, and we drank.

We were finishing dessert and were half way through the second glass of wine when I decided it was time to ask him about Giles Leonard.

"How is *Jesse's Secret* coming along?" I asked.

He frowned. "Slowly, I'm afraid. We've hit a bit of a snag."

"How so?"

"The author is not cooperating with the changes we've asked for. He's very uncommunicative, and we can never seem to find him. He sends us an occasional e-mail, but that's the only contact we've had with him."

"What about the agent? Can't he track him down?"

"There doesn't seem to be an agent. He sent the manuscript in over the transom. If it hadn't been addressed to me, it would still be sitting in the slush pile, but because I had only been at Pinnacle for a few weeks, and not that many people knew I was there, I didn't get many manuscripts coming just to me. When I saw the name *Jesse's Secret*, I remembered that you had mentioned it, and I assumed it was you who told him to send it to me."

I took a deep breath and decided it was time to tell him the whole story. I told him about Louisa Myner, and how she had first shown me the manuscript. And how I had praised it, and how happy she had been. I told him about Sam Pryor and the notebook he had shown me.

"And now they're both dead?" he asked.

I nodded. "Louisa drowned. An apparent suicide. Sam died in a house fire." I looked at the cheerfully crackling fire in the fireplace and shivered. "At least, that's what the police say."

"But you don't believe it?" he asked.

"Do you?"

"I- I don't know. It all seems too coincidental, and yet... I've seen Giles Leonard's work. His paintings are on the internet, and there are one or two in a gallery here. The paintings in *Jesse's Secret* were done by that same artist. Whoever he is."

I nodded. "I know. I agree. When I first heard about Louisa, I couldn't believe she would kill herself. But the more I talked to people, heard about her instability, heard what her brother said, I accepted it. When Sam first came to me, I thought he was probably in denial. He didn't want to believe that Louisa was half mad. Mad enough to steal a former lover's work. Or mad enough to kill herself."

"So Giles Leonard was a former lover of Louisa's?"

"Yes. According to her brother. And she slashed up one of his paintings in a gallery in DC. Why else would she do such a thing?"

"Unrequited love. She wouldn't be the first to do crazy things because of it."

"But then there's the notebook. I keep coming back to it, and I just can't explain it away. And the missing draft." And then I thought of something else. I slapped my forehead. "And the break-in," I said.

"Break-in?"

"Yes. I can't believe I never made the connection. Our house was broken into shortly after Louisa showed me her work. Our dog Paddington was poisoned. But the weird thing was, nothing was taken."

"You think someone was looking for the draft?" he asked.

I nodded. "And they found it later in my office at the Arts Center."

He considered this. "And Sam called you and said he had found Giles Leonard?"

"Yes. I was to meet him at his house. He had something to show me. But when I got there, he was gone. I saw a man leaving the house, and I found this in the driveway." I pulled out the silver pen with the initials GL.

"So you think the man leaving Sam Pryor's house was Giles Leonard?"

"I think it must be. I had seen him before near Louisa's house, shortly before she was found dead."

"Does your description of that man match the description of Giles Leonard?"

"No one seems to know what Giles Leonard looks like. And no one knows where to find him. I thought maybe you might be able to shed some light, but it seems you don't know much more than I do about his whereabouts."

"I'll do some checking. There must be a way to track him down. As I said, we need to find him too."

So we left it at that.

That night in my hotel room I tossed and turned on the strange bed. I should have been happy. Daniel loved Wellington, and Katharine had too when I met with her. But I had trouble falling asleep. I was cold one minute and hot the next, and in my dreams, when sleep finally came, I heard Louisa calling me from the bottom of a well. "*Jesse's Secret* is mine. Bring it to me." I had the manuscript in my hands, but before I could get it to her, it burst into flames.

An old truck was pulling away from the house. He hadn't seen that before. Where had that come from? he wondered. And who was driving? There were only three of them in there. He trained his binoculars on the truck as it moved up the drive. Just three. The girl? Was that the girl driving?

He ran to his car and started it up quickly. He followed the truck, staying pretty far behind, out of their sight, wondering when the girl had gotten her license. He didn't

*think she had, but she was driving anyway. He thought
about stopping them, pretending to be an off-duty cop, but
they might be too smart to buy that. Not the boys, but the
girl. He would like to get a close up look at her though.*

*Sometimes he thought it would be nice to live there with
them. A family. He'd never had a real family. Lou was all
he'd ever had, and now he didn't even have her. Watching
them made him feel as if they were his family. He wanted to
tell the girl he knew she was not supposed to be driving. To
admonish her, the way a father or an uncle might. But he
couldn't risk it.*

*They didn't go far. Just down to the Quik Shop. All three
of them went in, and came out a few minutes later with a
bag of stuff. The little boy had a candy bar, the older one
had a giant sub-meatball looked like, and the girl just had a
sports drink.*

*They headed back toward the house. He didn't think he
would watch them anymore tonight. Sarah was away.
There was nothing more he could find out till she came
back.*

Chapter Sixteen

I got home mid afternoon of the following day, and from the looks of things, everything had gone smoothly in my absence. It was the first time I had left the kids alone over night, and I had been anxious. I had alerted Marty and Skip that I would be away and asked them to keep an eye on things, and I had told the kids that if there was one hair out of place when I got back they wouldn't be left home alone again until Geordie was thirty five. They must have believed me. The place was relatively clean and tidy.

As I was fixing dinner the phone rang. I picked up and Dougie's calm twang said, "Hey, Sar. How'd your trip go?"

"Dougie, Hi. It was great. They loved *Wellington's Wand,* and have high hopes for big sales."

"That's great, darlin'. Just great. Our boy is dancing a jig up on some cloud."

"He is. He would like this one, I think."

"Now listen. I had my friend do some checking. Apparently Louisa Myner did go to art school. The Maryland Institute College of Art in Baltimore. She didn't graduate, but she was there three years. There was no record of a student named Giles Leonard though."

"Really? How odd."

"Now. Here's the other thing. We found a professor who remembers her. She's retired and lives in Annapolis. She said she'd be glad to talk to you, but she's hard of hearing and doesn't much like the phone, so you'd best come to see her."

"That's great, Dougie. I've been planning on going to DC anyway to talk to the folks who worked with Sam Pryor at his art agency. I'll go and see her on the way there."

"Good idea. We didn't find much on Giles Leonard. Just the stuff on the internet about his paintings. We're still checking though."

"Okay. Thanks, Dougie,"

"Oh, hey. I'm so glad you're finally using Tom's truck. When did Grace get her license?"

"What?"

"Uh oh."

"Dougie, Grace doesn't have her license. Just her learner's permit. We've talked about getting it tuned up, but as far as I know, Tom's truck hasn't moved in two years."

"Well, I might be hallucinating, but I swear I saw that truck come bouncing out of Doc's Quik Shop parking lot last evening. Grace was behind the wheel, Justin ridin' shotgun, and Geordie tucked in between them. I tell you, it was a sight for sore peepers. I thought how happy old Tom would have been if he could'a seen 'em."

"Yes, well, Grace has this problem of not being able to understand that a learner's permit is not a driver's license. I cannot believe she did that. And to take Justin and Geordie. And I was just thinking how mature she's been lately."

"Sarah, I don't think there's a red blooded kid on this planet who didn't drive with only a learner's once in while. Hell, Tom and me used to drive when we were fourteen, two years before we were legal."

"That was then; this is now, Dougie. I can't let them get away with that."

"Well, don't tell them I was the one who blew the whistle. And don't be too hard on them. The truck's back safely, and there's no harm done, right?"

"There might be some harm done when I get hold of them."

"They're great kids, Sarah. They wouldn't be normal if they didn't try it on now and then."

"Here comes Geordie. I better go. Thanks for checking on Louisa and Giles for me."

"Right, darlin'. I'll let you know if I find anything else."

We hung up just as Geordie came in the door. He raced to me and gave me a hug. "Hi, Mom. How was New York City? Did Mr. Hollister like the book?"

"He loved it. He thinks it has big sales potential."

"That's good, right?"

"Right. It's great. The bigger the sales, the richer we get."

"Good, Mom. That's so good."

"So what happened around here? Anything interesting?"

"Nope. Nothing. Just a regular night, except you were away." He pulled open the fridge, took out a quart of chocolate milk and poured himself a glass. "And Grace and Justin didn't even have a fight."

"Well, that's something new and different," I said. "Where'd that come from? I didn't buy any chocolate milk."

Geordie stopped mid sip. "Umm..." He shrugged noncommittally. "I forget."

He forgot? Good God, was I raising a politician?

"You forget? I think you've been watching too many Senate hearings," I said.

"Huh?"

"Let me guess. I bet it came from Doc's Quik Shop, right?"

Geordie searched for the right answer. "Maybe. I gotta go do homework." He finished his milk and put his glass in the sink.

Smart boy. Doing homework was usually a good way to get out of the witness stand. I decided to let him go. After all, it was Grace and Justin who should have known better. It wasn't Geordie's fault.

Later, when Grace and Justin were home circling the kitchen like sharks waiting for dinner, I brought it up again.

"So. I see you got some groceries," I said.

"Groceries?" Justin said, hopefully.

"Well, chocolate milk. Some cookies."

"Yeah. There wasn't any milk," Justin said.

Grace shot him a look.

"I gotta go do homework," he said, hoisting his new messenger bag.

When he left the kitchen, I looked at Grace. "So how does the truck drive?" I asked. "I'm surprised it started. It's been so long."

Grace shrugged. "It took a while to get it going. You said I could drive it, Mom."

"I meant after you had your license. You know that."

"I'll have it in three days, Mom. You said we could go on Saturday. That's in three days."

"Grace, what would have happened if you'd had an accident? Or if you'd been stopped by the police for some reason. Driving without a license is no joke."

"But I didn't get stopped. We got the milk and some other stuff and came right home. It was no big deal."

"Well, it's a big deal to me. You knew it was wrong, and you knew I was counting on you to behave responsibly."

"I did act responsibly. We were out of milk, and I went and got some. I don't see what's so terrible about that."

"Well, I'm disappointed. I feel that you took advantage of me."

"Mom, I didn't take advantage of you."

"You did, Gracey. I trusted you, and the minute I was gone you disobeyed me. Maybe you're not as grown up as I thought."

"Mom. I'm sorry. I didn't think it was that big a deal."

I said nothing. "Can I still get my license this Saturday?"

"I don't know, Grace. I'm going to have to think about this."

"Mom. I'm sorry. But we needed the milk. And it seemed dumb not to get it when the truck was right there, and I'm a perfectly good driver."

"You know how I feel about this, Grace. If you can't be trusted to obey the driving laws I'm not sure you're ready to drive."

Grace stormed off to her room and I stared out at the river, wishing I could ask Tom what he thought I should do.

Hollister had emailed him and indicated there was some problem with the manuscript. Wanted to know if Giles Leonard is a pseudonym, and asking for documentation that the work belongs to Giles Leonard. Just routine, Hollister had said. Made him wonder if the ditz had spilled something to him about Louisa Myner. Maybe she knew more that he thought she knew. He definitely had to keep her in his sights. She was the only potential problem right now, the only thing that stood between him and safety. And of course, the chance to finally make some real money. He had the whole stash of paintings, now, and the money he'd get from the book.

He also had the notebook, which he could show to Hollister as proof that the paintings were his.

Maybe he could even get Giles Leonard to come out of hiding again, once this all blew over. He could change his look. Spread the word that he had left the country because of Louisa. Because of how crazy she was, stalking him, slashing up the painting and all that. He could return and go back to the way it had been in the old days, before Louisa had changed her mind about all of it. Before she had broken their pact. Before she had screwed it all up.

He thought about her. How she had been when she was young. He missed that Louisa. The one who had listened to everything he said. The one who had trusted him and counted on him. He missed that Louisa, but he didn't miss the Louisa she had turned in to. The one who betrayed him. No. He didn't miss that one at all. In fact, he was glad she was gone. She had done nothing but stand in his way. He didn't miss her. And he didn't feel bad. It was all her fault. She just got what she deserved.

He'd be coming into money soon. He decided he could upgrade to a decent motel. He was sick of the crap place, and he needed a better place.

He took a swig from the bottle of bourbon beside his bed. Yes. Tomorrow he would get a better place and have a little celebration. He was a well known artist and pretty soon he would be a rich artist.

Chapter Seventeen

On Monday I went to see Louisa's neighbors and landlords, Ruth and Jerry Willet. I didn't want to stray far from the truth, so when I called to make an appointment to meet with them, I told them that I taught at the Arts Council, and I was trying to make sense of Louisa's death. I may have let them believe my acquaintance with her was greater than it was, and I didn't tell them everything about the manuscript, but they seemed happy enough to talk to me, and seemed to understand why I would want to find out what I could about her last weeks.

I arrived at their house at 11:00 AM, as we had agreed. They ushered me into the den where a fire was burning, offered me tea or coffee, and sat together on the couch, prepared to answer my questions.

"We were very fond of Louisa," Ruth said. "She was a lovely neighbor, and a wonderful tenant. I can't imagine anyone who could have taken better care of our little cottage."

"She lived here for how long?" I asked.

"It's been about three years now. A dear friend of ours worked with Louisa at the National Gallery in DC. She was very fond of her, and when Louisa said she wanted to move to the Eastern Shore, Mary called us to see if we might rent the cottage to her. Mary had been visiting us just a few weeks earlier, and I told her how sad I was that our tenant was leaving. He was a nice young man who taught math at Easton Middle School. He had decided to go back to school for his master's degree, and was moving to Baltimore.

"When Mary heard that Louisa was looking for a place, she called us. We liked her right away, and even though we heard that she'd had some problems, a breakdown of some sort, she seemed lovely. And Mary's an excellent judge of character, isn't she, dear?"

Jerry nodded vigorously. "Yes. Oh, yes. Mary wouldn't steer us wrong."

"So we agreed to let her rent the cottage, and as far as we knew, she was quite happy there. Until..."

"And there were never any problems?" I asked.

"None at all. She was very quiet. Not terribly sociable, you know. Kept to herself mostly. But she kept herself busy. Worked at her job at the Harriet Tubman Museum down in Cambridge. Went out rowing in her little boat. And she loved to go biking."

"And she had a young man who came around," Jerry added. "Sam, his name was. Very pleasant chap he was."

"And of course, her brother visited her now and then," Ruth went on. "Poor soul. Very cut up he was about it all."

"And the museum in Cambridge?" I asked. "You said it was the Harriet Tubman Museum?"

"That's right."

"Did she ever mention a man named Giles Leonard to you?"

"Giles Leonard. Giles Leonard. I believe that's the name of the artist she was involved with at one time."

"I think that's right," I said. "Do you know anything about him? Did she ever talk much about him?"

They both looked thoughtful. Then Jerry said, "I don't believe I ever heard Louisa mention him. Did you, love?"

Ruth said cautiously, "Louisa never spoke of him to me, but I did hear some, well, rumors. They say she slashed up a picture of his. One that was hanging in an art gallery in DC."

"Yes. I heard that too. But she never said anything about him to you? Never mentioned where he lives or anything?"

"She never spoke of him. I think she was trying to put it all behind her, if you know what I mean. I'm sure she didn't want to be reminded of that...difficult time," Ruth said.

"And Louisa seemed fine to you? She didn't seem unstable, or depressed?"

They both shook their heads. "She seemed as healthy as you or me," Jerry said.

"We were both as shocked as we could be when we heard what had happened to her. We still can't believe it. Can we, love?"

Jerry shook his head. "Such a damn waste. It's something we'll never understand."

"I keep asking myself if there was something we could have done. Had her over to dinner, been more neighborly, you know. But she was such a private person. We didn't want to intrude."

"I don't think there was anything anyone could have done," I said. "She was ill, and her illness finally got the best of her."

They both nodded, and after a bit of small talk, I was about to take my leave when Ruth said, "She did give us a number where we could reach her during the day, if you'd like that. It was different from the museum number for some reason. I think I still have it if you want it." She went to her desk and returned with a card which she handed to me.

"Thank you." I looked at the card there was a Cambridge area code and phone number written on it, and the name Al. I didn't think it would help much, but Ruth seemed so eager to help, so I put it in my wallet and stood up to go.

When he saw where she was heading he couldn't believe it. Could not believe it. He'd been at his post that morning, first time in a while. He'd taken a few days off. Now that he'd moved to a nicer place he didn't mind being there, and he was beginning to feel a bit calmer about everything. The D.C. cops had ruled the fire an accident, so he was good on that one. And he'd talked to Hollister. Actually talked to him. That had been a kick. He hadn't been Giles in a long while. It felt good. He was going to meet with him next week. He could pull this off, piece of cake. He'd done it before and he could do it again. He would show Hollister the notebook. He would tell him he was working on a big new show. Tell him he wanted the book to stay like it was- no changes. He could pull the whole artistic integrity thing- don't you dare meddle with my work. My work is my soul, and it stays as it is blah blah blah. He had heard Louisa pull that crap enough times back in the old days when he had suggested changes to make her stuff more sellable.

So it was all good. And now this. Jesus.

She just couldn't let it go. He thought she'd have dropped it by now, but she just had to keep snooping and sniffing like a damned hound dog. What, she think she's some kind of female detective- or maybe that writer who thought she could solve mysteries. Jesus.

It was odd for her to go out in the car in the morning. Usually she worked in the morning and went out later. So he'd been surprised when she got in the car soon after the kids left for school. And even more surprised when she'd headed away from town. He felt the first twinge of fear right about then. She was headed out towards Hopkins Neck. Out towards Lou's place. Don't be stupid, he told himself. Why would she do that? Lou's not there, she knows that. And the place has been all cleaned out. They said they weren't going to rent it again. One of their grandkids might want to stay there they said. The road leads to plenty of other places besides Lou's.

But she kept going. Making all the turns that led to Lou's, and finally turned right into the drive. He couldn't help himself. He had to follow her, even though it was dangerous.

She drove right on past Lou's and pulled up in front of the landlords' place. What did she want with those two old farts? Was she grilling them about Louisa? Jesus. What was wrong with this woman?

He turned around in Louisa's driveway and went back out on Hopkins Road, parked down a ways, out of sight, and waited until she came out, almost an hour later.

Followed her back into to town, picked up a new bottle of bourbon, then back to his place to think. And drink.

He told himself that, right now, there was no way she could prove anything. And unless she found out about the studio, she wouldn't be able to figure it out. And how could she find out about that? No one knew about it but him. And Al Dugan, of course. But how would she find him? No. there was no need to panic. Not yet anyway.

Chapter Eighteen

The following day I drove down to Cambridge. It was a beautiful day, though cold and blustery, and I decided I would take Paddington with me, and take her for a walk through Blackwater Wildlife Refuge. It was the third week in November. Thanksgiving was only a week away. The trees were mostly bare now, but the river was bright blue and the shore grass was golden. The geese were everywhere, honking and squawking and looking for food and shelter from the cold, like creatures everywhere.

Paddington and I spent a happy hour meandering through the Blackwater hiking trails, and then I continued on towards Cambridge. I found the Harriet Tubman Museum, a tiny storefront Museum on Ridge Street. I left Paddington in the car, assuring her I wouldn't be long, and leaving the window open just a crack. Then I went into the museum to make my inquiries.

There was a woman giving a tour to a group of school children, and I assumed that that was what Louisa did as well. I shopped in the little store attached to the museum, waiting for the tour to be over so I could talk to the woman.

Finally she finished up and the children filled the gift shop, and I went back into the museum part of the building and up to the tour giver.

"Hello," I said. "I wonder if you might be able to help me."

"I'll sure try, hon. What can I do for you?"

"I'm looking for information about a former employee. A Louisa Myner? I just wanted to speak with anyone who might have known her.

"Louisa Myner? Hmm. Doesn't sound familiar. How long ago was she here?"

"I believe she was here for about three years, up until about six weeks ago."

"Louisa Myner." The little woman shook her head. "Doesn't ring any bells. And I know pretty much everyone here. Most of us are volunteers see. Except for the girls in the shop. But they're all work study students from Cambridge High. Was she a young girl?"

"No no. Maybe I'm mistaken about the museum. Are there any others in town?"

The woman considered for a minute. "Well, there's the Historical Society. But it's tiny. Not a real museum. This is the biggest one we have here. We have a nice size library though. Could she have worked there maybe?"

"Maybe that's it," I said, though I didn't think it was.

Back in the car I stroked Paddington absently, and thought about why Louisa would lie about where she worked. Was she embarrassed? What kind of job could she have had?

I remembered the phone number with the Cambridge exchange, and I called it on my cell phone.

"Yo. This is Al."

"Hi, Al, my name is Sarah Landing. I was a friend of Louisa Myner's."

"Yeah?"

"You knew her, I believe."

"Yeah. I knew her a bit. She rented a room from me."

"She rented a room?"

"Sure did."

"Look, Al, could I talk to you in person? I'm trying to understand some things about how and why she died. Could you possibly meet me somewhere?"

"I work at the Hyatt. I don't get off for a while, but you come over here and I'll talk to you. Louisa was a nice lady. She shouldn't have died."

"Where will I find you?"

126

"I'll be in the fitness center. Just ask for Al."

It must have been a down time at the Hyatt fitness center, because Al was the only person in there. He was sitting behind the check-in desk, reading a newspaper.

"I'm looking for Al," I said, when I entered the center.

"You found him," he said. "Al Dugan, at your service." He held out his hand. "You the lady who called?" he asked.

"Yes. I called about Louisa Myner."

"Have a seat." He motioned to a chair beside the desk. I sat down.

"What did you say your name was?" he asked.

"Sarah Landing."

"And you were Louisa's friend, huh?" He asked.

"Yes," I told him. I didn't feel the need to explain any more than that. "You said she rented a room from you?"

"Yeah, but she didn't live there. She just painted there. She was learning to paint. Taking classes somewhere, and using my room as a studio. She didn't want anyone to know, she said, because she was worried she wouldn't be any good. I never told anyone, but now it doesn't matter, I guess. Does it?"

"I don't think she would mind you telling me, Al."

He shrugged. "Anyway, she shouldn't have worried about it. She was good."

"You saw her work?" I asked excitedly.

"I saw some of her paintings about six months after she started renting the place from me. I went up there, just to make sure everything was all right. See, I heard voices. A man and a woman. They were arguing. I couldn't hear much, just some raised voices, shouting. Mostly the man, but I couldn't make out what he was saying. Something like if it hadn't been for him she'd have nothing.

"Then I heard her say, 'Go ahead then. Take them.' Then I heard a car drive out, so I guess he left. A little while later, I heard her car drive out."

"Do you know who the man was? Would you recognize him if you saw him?"

"I never got a look at him. See, the entrance to the garage apartment is on the other side, and so I never saw him. She never mentioned him, and I never asked. Didn't want her to think I'd been eavesdropping, you know."

"So when did you see her paintings?"

"Well it was later that same night. I just felt uneasy. I wanted to make sure everything was all right up there. And, truth be told, I was curious. This man was taking her pictures, well, I wanted to see what it was he was taking."

"This was after she had left for the day?" I asked.

He nodded. "I waited until I knew she was gone for the night. She never came back at night. Sometimes she would leave during the day, go and get some lunch I guess, but she was never there at night. I hardly ever saw her because I was at work over here most days. But I get one week day off a week cause I have to work one weekend day.

"Anyway, I went up the stairs and unlocked her door with my key. It was the first time I'd been inside that room since she had moved there. She didn't have much in there. A table and a chair. A bench that was full of paints. A bunch of canvases, and an easel with a half done painting on it. Leaning against the wall were other paintings, lots of them. I don't know much about art, but I could tell that these were good. They were real good."

I took out the post card with the Giles Leonard paintings, and the paintings I had gotten from the Giles Leonard web site.

"Do they look anything like these?" I asked.

Al took the post card and the papers and studied them carefully. "That's one of them I think," he said, indicating the post card that Sam had shown me.

"What happened to Louisa's things?" I asked. "After she died?"

"That was the weirdest thing. Once I heard about her death, I didn't know what to do with her things. But when I went up to the apartment, it was almost empty. All her canvases, and her paintings and easel, they were all gone. Only thing left was the stuff that had been there before. The old table and chair. And the bench. Everything else was gone."

"So you didn't know she had left?"

He shook his head. "Not until I heard about her death. It made me real sad. Specially after she gave me her painting and all."

"She gave you one?"

128

He nodded. "It was just about six months ago. I ran into her as I was coming home and she was leaving. 'How's the painting going?' I asked her. She seemed different. Happier than the last time I'd seen her, and I don't know, just happier mostly.

"She said her painting was going well and asked would I like to see them. I told her I sure would.

"So we went up and she had about ten canvases, some big, some smaller, and they were beautiful. Like I said, I don't know much about art, but I could tell these were real good. I knew my girl friend would like them. She's always going on about art and things. So I said, 'How much do you charge for one of them?'

"'For you, Al?' she asked me.

"'Well, I'll be giving it to Eileen,' I says.

"'Pick one,' she told me. 'It's yours.'

"So I picked one of a little boy, sitting on a step in front of his house. You can't exactly tell that's what it is. It's sort of what they call impression-like, if you know what I'm saying."

I nodded. I knew exactly what he was saying. I'd seen what sounded like the same painting in the pages of *Jesse's Secret*.

He woke up in a fog, head pounding. The new bottle was empty, and the clock had to be lying. He could not have slept past noon. Damn. He should have been at his post. He needed to watch her. If she was going to pull this amateur detective crap he had to keep her in his sights.

He wondered if he should do one of those cheesy notes, telling her to butt out. But that would probably just feed her curiosity. Besides, did anyone really do that shit except in dime store novels? Jesus. What was he doing, still here playing spy, still afraid, still paying for Louisa's stupidity.

Louisa and that stupid ditzy bitch. Jesus.

Well, today was a lost one. He felt too sick to do anything but lie there and stare at the idiot box.

Tomorrow he'd get back to his post.

Chapter Nineteen

I now knew that Louisa had been the artist, not Giles Leonard. Had she threatened to expose him? Was that why he had killed her?

I was on my way to Annapolis, my mind racing with the things I had learned from Al Dugan the day before. I had an appointment to speak with Penelope Barnes, Louisa Myner's former art teacher. I was to meet her at 11:00 a.m. at her house on Lowell Street.

I drove through the twisty little streets in the historic district of Annapolis until I found Lowell Street, and came to number 12. It was a tiny cottage right on the banks of the Severn River.

It was precisely 11:00 when I rang the bell. I heard a rumbling noise, slowly growing in intensity, like a train pulling into the station. I peered through the window beside the door and saw that it wasn't a train but two large Old English Sheep dogs and a Bassett hound, bounding towards the door. Behind them came a woman whom I presumed to be Penelope Barnes.

"Get back, get back!" she commanded, hauling the largest of dogs away from the door and flinging him towards the back end of the hallway. "Go to your beds," she said, in a voice that was clearly meant to be obeyed. The dogs slunk away and disappeared through the door.

Though she was tiny, and must have been in her early seventies, Penelope Barnes was clearly a force to be reckoned with. She had short white hair, warm blue eyes, and an intelligent face. She was small and slender and dressed more like a college student than a retired art professor. She wore stylish, well fitting jeans and a long, multi-colored poncho over a black turtle neck.

She opened the door, and said, "Ms. Landing?"

"Yes. Sarah."

"I'm Penelope Barnes. Come in." She stepped back, opening the door wider. "Sorry about the welcome committee. The door bell acts like an adrenalin rush to them."

"My dog's the same way," I told her.

"What kind?" she asked.

"A Chesapeake."

"Ah. They're so sweet."

"Yes, Paddington is very sweet. Not the sharpest tack in the box, but very sweet."

She led me out of the tiny hall into a large room that had a glorious view of the Severn. The room took up the entire downstairs of her house, except for the little entrance hall. In the far corner of the room, the three dogs sat panting on their dog beds. In the corner opposite that was a tiny kitchen with playhouse sized appliances. The long wall in front of us was all glass, and the wall behind us, paintings, easels, canvases, some hanging, some stacked, some being worked on. In the middle of the room, a long pine table and several chairs, and in the last corner, a wood burning stove, two comfortable looking overstuffed chairs and a sofa. Bookshelves lined both the other two walls. It seemed a perfect house for her. I was charmed by it.

She led me to the comfortable corner and indicated that I should sit. I sat. There was something about her that made one do exactly as she said. No wonder the dogs had obeyed so quickly.

"Can I get you a cup of tea?" she asked.

"That would be lovely," I said.

I sat in the comfortable chair, the heat from the wood stove soothing, and I watched the river. I felt I could have stayed there forever.

Penelope brought a tray with two cups, a tea pot, and a plate of thinly sliced date-nut bread spread with cream cheese. "I know it's not tea time, but it's elevenses, as they say in England, and that will do just as well."

"This is a wonderful house," I said

"It suits me very well," she said. "I have everything I need, and not too much that I don't. Just the way I like it."

The tea was delicious, and the date bread even better. I told her so.

"So. You were a friend of Louisa Myner's?" she asked.

"Yes. Well, actually, she had signed up to take my course."

"And what do you teach?" she asked.

I explained about my picture book class, and told her the whole story of how I had met Louisa. "She showed me her picture book manuscript, and I was so impressed. It's called *Jesse's Secret*. It's beautiful. I knew it could be published. I was terribly disappointed when she didn't show up for my class. I tried to contact her, but she didn't return my calls. I even drove out to see her. Then, about three weeks after I had met her, I heard that she was dead."

"Yes. Doug Firth told me. I'm so sorry. She was a lovely person. And very talented. I hadn't seen her in years, of course, but I was very sorry to hear about it. Doug said that there is some question about whether or not her death was accidental or a suicide?"

"Well, that's why I wanted to see you. You see, there is some question about whether *Jesse's Secret* really was Louisa's."

"What do you mean?"

I explained about Giles Leonard, and Louisa's instability. "Do you know a man named Sam Pryor?"

"The art dealer?"

"Yes."

"I've met him once or twice. And, of course, I know him from his reputation. He's a wonderful dealer."

"Well, Sam and Louisa were having a relationship. Sam did not believe that Louisa had killed herself. And he was positive that *Jesse's Secret* was hers."

"And did you agree with him?"

"Initially, I was skeptical. I felt that he was in denial. That he didn't want to admit that Louisa was depressed, unstable, suicidal. But then Sam called and said he had more proof that *Jesse's Secret* was Louisa's. He asked me to meet him the next afternoon at his house in Oxford. I drove over there and waited, but he didn't show up. A few days later I heard he was dead."

"Yes. I heard about that. A house fire, wasn't it?"

"That's right."

"Do the police suspect arson?"

"No. They think it was an accident."

"But you don't believe that?"

"Not anymore. I did some checking and found out some things. There's still a lot I don't understand, but I know enough to believe that Louisa was the artist and writer of *Jesse's Secret*. What I don't know is why Giles Leonard, whoever he is, has claimed it."

"Probably for the age old reason: money."

"You taught Louisa at MICA, didn't you?"

"I did. She was an excellent student."

"Why didn't she finish her degree?"

"I have no idea. She did finish three years. She was very talented. I thought maybe she had gone to Europe and studied there. I lost track of her when she left MICA, but I do remember her well, and I remember that she was very talented."

"Did you ever know Giles Leonard?"

"I don't remember anyone by that name, but I taught a lot of students over the years. I don't remember all of them, so it's possible I met him and forgot him."

"Did you know any friends of Louisa's? Anyone who might know why she left?"

Penelope thought for a minute. "No one comes to mind. Louisa was quiet. Very unassuming and shy. She loved to paint, and she had talent, but she wasn't particularly interested in showing her work, or in developing a career for herself."

We talked a little while longer and I finished my tea and ate way too much of the delicious date nut bread.

As I was leaving she said, "Please let me know when *Jesse's Secret* is available. I want to get a copy," she said.

"I'll send you one," I promised.

An hour and a half later I was at Sam Pryor's art dealership and gallery, Ludlow and Pryor. This gallery was serious. It was on the top floor of the Waxter building, a large office building that seemed more suitable to a bank than an art gallery. There was a reception area, with a desk behind which sat a receptionist who was efficiently fielding phone calls in a polite but no nonsense sort of way.

After the third call she turned to me. "Can I help you?"

"I'm Sarah Landing. I have an appointment with Mr. Ludlow."

"Oh, yes, Ms. Landing. Let me tell him you're here."

"Ms. Landing is here, Graham."

A minute later I saw Giles Leonard, or at least the person I had convinced myself was Giles Leonard coming down the hall to greet me, complete with Armani suit and grey ponytail.

"Ms. Landing? I'm Graham Ludlow," he said, shaking my hand coolly.

"Sarah Landing," I managed to stutter, still in shock.

"Let's go back to my office. He lead me down the hall past paintings so beautiful I wanted to stop and gape, but Graham/Giles was having none of it, and I practically had to run to keep up with him.

His office, like the rest of the building was modern. Snowy white carpet, so plush I could have stretched out and had a little nap. A black steel desk, the kind that made you wonder where he kept his stuff. There was nothing on it but a phone and a computer monitor and keyboard. The wall behind him was glass with a breathtaking view of the Potomac. But it was the other three walls that I stared at. On the right, a Jasper Johns. On the left, a Rauschenberg, and behind me, next to the door, a Roy Lichtenstein. They were all the real thing. Not prints. Not copies. Real. Originals.

I stared, wide eyed, quivering with excitement, like a dog in a butcher shop. I took some deep breaths and tried to pretend I came face to face with art like this on a regular basis.

"You were a friend of Sam's?" he said.

I nodded. "I've known him for years. We were at Georgetown University together."

He shook his head. "I still can't believe he's gone. It's just...incomprehensible."

"You were close?"

"We've been business partners for 15 years. And friends through it all. That doesn't happen very often."

"You must miss him terribly. I'm so sorry."

He smiled a sad half smile, which made him seem much more human. "I'm still surprised when I see his empty office. The other day one of our artists called for him. He hadn't heard what had happened. I almost transferred the call. It's crazy."

"No it's not. When my husband died, it was months before I stopped expecting him to walk in the door every night around six o'clock."

"You lost your husband?"

"Three years ago. A car accident."

"I'm so sorry. That's a whole other level of hell."

I nodded. "Will you keep the gallery?" I asked.

"I'm still sorting all that out. His son is an artist. He may want to come into the business. But I'll need someone else in the meantime." He sighed. "We were a good team. I'm good at business and sales side of things. Sam had the vision. He really knew which artists had it and which didn't. He could spot talent a mile away."

I thought of what Sam had said about Louisa's work. I was more convinced than ever that he had been right.

"So anyway, how can I help you?" he asked. He picked up a silver pen and tapped his palm with it. A nervous habit. I stared at the pen. It was identical to the one I had found. That one I thought had belonged to Giles Leonard. GL. Graham Ludlow.

I pulled the pen out of my purse. "Does this by any chance belong to you?"

He took the pen. "It does indeed. Where did you find it?"

I told him and he said, "Yes. I had been on the shore that day. We have a few big clients down there, and I was making a sales call. I stopped at Sam's to see if he wanted to take me fishing, but he wasn't home. I was going to leave him a note, but I decided I'd just leave a message on his cell. I must have dropped the pen then."

"I'm sorry to see you've replaced it already," I said.

"No. Actually, this one is Sam's. Or was. One of our artists gave each of us one for Christmas last year. We were always getting them mixed up." He held the pen out to me, and I saw that it was identical except that the initials were S P. "Thank you for returning my pen. But surely that can't be the only reason for your trip?"

"No, I- I wanted to ask you about something," I paused, "but I'm not sure how to begin."

"Close your eyes and jump, as my father used to say."

"Okay. First let me ask, did you know Sam's friend Louisa Myner?" I thought he must have known her because I had seen him at her house that day.

He leaned back in his seat and half turned towards the window, gazing out at the city below.

"Yes. I knew Louisa, but not very well. I had only met her maybe three or four times. And most of those times were brief. She was at Sam's house one time when he and I came back from fishing. A few times I was here in the office when she came up to have dinner with Sam. Once I had a drink with them. I went to her house one time when Sam and I were going fishing. I talked to her briefly then. And one time I went over there because Sam asked me to, but she wasn't there. He was away at the time, and hadn't been able to reach her. He was worried about her. Rightly so, as it turned out. It was just a few days later that they found her body. "

"Yes. I saw you there that day," I told him. "I had driven out too, for quite the same reason. I had been trying to reach her and had had no luck."

He looked surprised. "Did we meet? I think I would have remembered if we had."

"No. I was in my car, and I passed you as I was driving out."

He nodded thoughtfully. "When I didn't find Louisa in her cottage that day, I went up to the big house to see if they knew where she was. They said they thought she was in Maine. She went every summer, and her little boat was gone. She usually loaned it to a boy who lives up the creek away, in exchange for him cutting her grass and watering her garden." He said the last words almost as if he were quoting verbatim. "It's funny, I remember exactly what she told me, because it was just a few days later that I heard about her death. I couldn't believe it. Sam was still away. I tried to reach him, but by that time he had left Italy and was in Morocco. His cell phone didn't work there, and I didn't have much of an itinerary for him. I didn't want to contact his family because Sam was pretty hush hush about Louisa. He'd been separated quite a while, but his wife was still fighting the divorce."

He stared up at the Rauschenberg as if it gave him strength. "Sam was devastated. By the time he got home, she'd already been buried. He went up to Maine, but..."

"Yes. I know. He came to talk to me, shortly after he got back. About *Jesse's Secret*. Did he tell you about it?"

"Was that the picture book? Louisa's book?"

"Yes."

"He mentioned it before he went away. He was excited for her. Thought it was terrific." He shrugged. "I don't remember hearing much about it after he came back and found out what had happened."

"Did he ever mention a man named Giles Leonard?"

"Giles Leonard? The artist?"

"You know him?"

"I know his work, slightly. He hasn't done much in the last few years though."

"Did Sam ever talk to you about him?"

"He asked me if we could get some contact information on him. He didn't say what he wanted it for. It was right before he went to Maine, after Louisa died."

"Did Sam ever say anything to you about Louisa being worried about something before she died? Or about his belief that she didn't commit suicide?"

"Not in so many words, though I knew he was having trouble coming to grips with it. I think he may have blamed himself for not being here, for not seeing the signs of her instability."

I didn't want to say too much here. For one thing, I had promised both Sam and Greg that I wouldn't. They both felt strongly that Louisa's privacy was important. Besides that, I didn't know this man well and wasn't sure if I could trust him. Maybe it was because of my initial wrong impression that he was Giles Leonard, even though I now knew he wasn't, but for some reason I just couldn't trust him completely.

"Were you worried about Sam? Before he died, I mean? The police report said he'd been drinking heavily the night of the fire. I didn't know Sam that well, but I've never thought of him as a heavy drinker. Had he started drinking more as a result of Louisa's death?"

Again, Graham stared at the Rauschenberg as if the answer to my question was written there. "I didn't see anything to make me believe he had a drinking problem, though he did drink. But there was something going on with him. He wasn't himself at all. I put it down to sadness and guilt over Louisa's death. And I still think that. He may have had one too many that night, and forgot to close the screen in front of his fireplace. It wouldn't be the first time it's happened."

I nodded. There was nothing more I could find out from this man. I made getting ready to leave motions, expecting that he'd be glad to see the last of me. But instead of jumping up and ushering me out, he gave me a quizzical look and said, "So what is your involvement in all of this?" he asked. "You don't strike me as the type to go in for private investigations."

"You've got that right," I said. "I never had aspirations along those lines." Should I tell him all about *Jesse's Secret*, Giles Leonard, Louisa's hidden studio? I decided not to. "It's a very long story, and I'm not really at liberty to go into it all right now. But if and when I fill in the details, I promise I'll tell you the whole story."

He stood up and I did too. "I'd appreciate that," he said. "Here's my card. Call me when you get your answers."

"I will," I thought. But at the rate I was going I wasn't sure I would ever get my answers.

Christ, the bitch was chocking up the miles. Annapolis and then DC. Don't know who she was seeing in Annapolis, maybe not even related to Louisa, but in DC it was Ludlow and Pryor, and her reason there seemed pretty self evident.

Why? Why was she doing this to him? What was it with these bitches that they had to torture him like this? Just like Louisa. Like they wanted to stick it to him. Just couldn't let him be.

God, Lou. He missed her. He did. He had to admit it, he missed her. Even though he had mostly hated her in the last few years, he still missed her. Strange. But it was the old Lou he missed. The young Lou. God they had had fun. And she had understood him. Known everything about him. And he about her. Yeah, he missed her. She was all he had. All he had ever had, if the truth be told. But it wasn't too late for him. He'd have money soon. He could make a new life for himself. Start all over again. Maybe he'd even start painting again himself.

But he was getting plenty tired of this game. She better let it go soon, or he was going to have to do something. He didn't want to. Any more than he had wanted to put an end to Lou's shit. But if they drove him to it, was else could he do?

Maybe he should pay a visit to Al Dugan himself? Just to be on the safe side.

Chapter Twenty

All the way home I felt deflated. I was no closer to finding Giles Leonard, or to understanding Louisa Myner. I thought about what Graham Ludlow had asked me. Why was I so interested in all of this? What answers was I looking for?

I wanted to know what had happened to Louisa, and what had happened to Sam. I wanted to know who Giles Leonard was, why he was claiming Louisa's book as his own. Why Louisa had a hidden studio in Cambridge, and why she had lied about it. Did I really believe that both Louisa and Sam had been murdered? If so why? And by whom?

Louisa had been dead for almost two months, and the sad truth of it was I had no more idea what had happened to her, or why than I had when I first heard about her death. And now that Sam was dead there wasn't even anyone else who really cared about the truth. They all just wanted to believe that Louisa was an unstable woman who was obsessed by a lover of ten years ago. So obsessed that she stole his work and pretended it was her own, and then took her own life. And that Sam had been so distraught by her death that he had drunk himself into oblivion and burned himself up.

But I didn't believe that. I couldn't let it go, but I couldn't think where else to look.

And, actually, there was one other person. Daniel. He needed to find Giles Leonard as much as I did, and he needed to find out who the real author of *Jesse's Secret* was, and where the sequel was.

As soon as I got home, I e-mailed Daniel, asking him if he had had any luck finding out the whereabouts of Giles Leonard. I also told him about finding Louisa's studio, and a little about what Al Dugan had told me. Then, up in my office I started drawing, sketching out an idea I'd had for a new book. As always, when I was drawing and it was going well, I lost all track of time, and before I knew it I heard the key in the door and Grace and Geordie were banging around downstairs. I heard a deeper male voice as well. Not Justin's. Hmmm.

"Hi Mom," Geordie called. "Where are you?"

"In my office. I'll be right down."

I was putting my work away when Geordie burst through my door, fizzing with excitement. "Mom! Grace has a boyfriend," he announced.

"She does?"

He nodded. "And he's *here*."

"Does the boyfriend have a name?" I asked.

Geordie nodded. "Connor. He was in the truck with her when they came to pick me up."

I had finally decided to let Grace take her driver's test the previous Saturday, provided she agreed to sign up for the safe driver's class for new drivers at the Y, and I had to admit, it was nice to have another driver in the family.

"Is he nice?" I asked.

Geordie thought about this. "Well, he's a lot nicer than Grace. He bought me a Twix bar at Doc's."

"I guess I better come and meet him."

"Yeah."

We went downstairs where I found Grace and a boy sitting on the couch in the den watching the "Daily Show."

"Hi, sweetie," I said. "Thanks for picking Geordie up."

"Hi, Mom. No problem." Then, as if she had just noticed him, she said, "Oh. This is Connor Shanagan."

The boy leapt up as I came into the room, which earned him more points than the Twix bar in my estimation.

"Hello, Connor." I shook his hand and said, "Don't get up," even though he was already up.

"Hi, Mrs. Landing," he said, and then resumed his seat, but rather than sitting right next to Grace as he had been before he squeezed himself against the opposite arm, as far away from her as he could get, apparently wishing to signal to me that he had no improper designs on my daughter.

I was not worried. I had full confidence in Grace's ability to take care of herself in this regard. I found myself agreeing with Geordie. This boy was probably a lot nicer than Grace, who could be somewhat heartless when it came to high school boys. At least, she enjoyed putting on a show of heartlessness.

"Do you go to school with Grace?" I asked.

"He's a senior," Grace said. Connor nodded.

"And he works at Firestone. He can get us a deal on new tires," Grace said. Again the boy nodded.

"Well, that's great," I said.

Grace hit the remote and turned the TV off. "Come on. I'll drive you home."

"Cool," he stood up. "Nice to meet you Mrs. Landing,"

"Nice meeting you, Connor."

"See ya, dude," he said to Geordie.

"Can I come?" Geordie asked.

Before they could answer I said, "You stay here with me. I want to hear about the play and everything. And besides, Paddington needs a little walk. Let's go down to the dock."

Grace and Connor made their escape, and Geordie and I walked down to the dock and watched Paddington chase the geese, and then stand on the end of the dock sniffing the air. It was dusk, and the sky was a palette of pinks and reds and purples. "Red in the night, sailor's delight. Red in the morning, sailors take warning," I said.

Geordie nodded. "It's going to be nice tomorrow."

A sharp wind blew in off the water, and we turned as one and headed back to the house. As we walked, Geordie gave me a lengthy report on the progress of the play, which was to take place the following week.

Back in the house I started dinner, and Justin came in. "Grace has a boyfriend." Geordie informed him as soon as he walked in.

"Boyfriend? Since when?" Justin asked.

"His name is Connor Shanagan. How do you know he's her boyfriend, Geordie? Maybe he's just a friend," I said.

Geordie shook his head. "They were holding hands," he said, making a gagging motion.

"He goes to the high school?" Justin said, though it came out came out sounding like e o oo ighoo because his mouth was full of a hot meatball he had stolen from the stove.

I nodded. "He's a senior. And he works at Firestone."

"He can get us free tires," Geordie said.

"Not free. Just a deal."

"Cool."

Grace returned. Dinner was almost ready when the phone rang. Geordie picked it up, and I heard him say, "Yes, sir. It's all better. I got my cast off a few weeks ago." Then, "I loved it. I thought it was the best of all." Another pause, and then "No, we're not. She's right here. Mom. For you." Geordie passed me the phone, and I heard Daniel's clipped British accent saying, "Sarah? I hope I'm not interrupting your dinner?"

"No, no. We haven't started yet."

"I'm glad. I got your e-mail, and I wanted to fill you in on an interesting development. I got a call from Giles Leonard. Apparently he's coming back to the states, and he wants to meet with me next week. He says he can prove beyond a shadow of doubt that the work is his."

"What? But..."

Then I heard Grace scream, "The sauce!" and race into the kitchen.

"Oops," I said. "I think our dinner is burning. I better go, but I have some things to tell you too. Can you call me tomorrow?"

"Of course. Talk to you then."

"Thanks, Daniel."

I put the phone down and made a dash for the kitchen, but Grace had gotten there first and seemed to have things pretty much in hand.

143

"Everything okay?" I asked. "Thanks for rescuing things."

"Some of the meat balls got burnt."

"Not to worry. Paddington will eat them.

"Yeah, and if Paddington won't, Justin will," Grace said.

After dinner I read to Geordie and got him into bed. I went back downstairs to let Paddington out, and as I waited for her, I watched the moon rising, leaving a shimmering yellow trail across the black river. A yellow brick road, I thought. Perhaps it would lead to Oz. These thoughts lead me back to my new story. It would be the story of a journey, I decided. A sea journey, perhaps, or a river trip. Paddington scratched at the door, shaking me out of my reverie. I let her in and we went upstairs to bed.

It was late when I noticed the message light on my phone blinking. I listened and heard Al Dugan's voice. "Mrs. Landing, Al Dugan here. About Louisa Myner. I thought of something that might help. I'll try you tomorrow."

That night I dreamed that I was drawing and drawing, filling paper after paper, but each time I finished a page it left my desk and floated out the window, and I was somehow unable to stop them. I watched my pages floating away, fluttering in the wind and growing smaller and smaller until I couldn't see them anymore. And no one would ever know they were mine, I thought. And that was the worst part of it all.

Chapter Twenty-One

The following morning I went to work on my new book as soon as I got the kids off. I worked for a few hours and then, feeling the need for some exercise, I snapped Paddington's leash on her and we headed out for a walk. We had been walking for about forty minutes when my cell phone rang.

What fresh hell? I thought, pulling it out of my jacket pocket. I didn't recognize the number, but it could be one of the kids' teachers, the school nurse, who knew.

I snapped it open. "Hello."

"Mrs. Landing?"

"Yes."

"This is Al Dugan. You came about Louisa Myner?"

"Yes, of course, Al. What's up?" I remembered the message he had left last night on the landline.

"I just wanted to tell you that it was Louisa's brother who took the paintings away that time. He called the other day. Said he was taking care of her estate and wondering if she had owed me anything. I recognized his voice."

I said nothing for a minute. I was trying to make sense of this.

"Mrs. Landing?" Al said.

"Y-yes. I'm still here. Are you, are you sure? "

"I'm right sure, ma'am. See, I realized when I heard him the other day that he has an accent very much like Mrs.

Myner had. And I remember that when he was shouting at her, his accent became even more pronounced."

And then the full impact of this hit me. Greg had lied again and again. He knew all about Louisa's art.

I thanked Al and hung up, my mind racing. It all came clear to me then. Of course. Greg Myner was Giles Leonard. He had been claiming Louisa's art for years.

I hurried back to the house. I had to call Daniel and tell him. Then I had to call the police.

I let myself in and ran upstairs to my office. I was half way across the room before I noticed him. Greg Myner was sitting on the stool at my drawing table, holding the drawings for my new picture book in one hand and a gun in the other.

I had seen rifles before, and shot guns, but I think that was the first time I had ever seen an actual hand gun outside of a policeman's holster. It was definitely the first time I had ever had one pointed at me. I had never imagined that having a gun pointed at me would be a barrel of laughs, no pun intended, but neither had I imagined how utterly horrifying, how completely petrifying it was. I was paralyzed. I couldn't speak. I couldn't move. I couldn't think.

"Hello, Sarah," he said. "Have a seat, why don't you?" he nodded toward the desk chair.

My legs shook as I made it to the chair and dropped heavily into it. I stared down at the floor as if there was a secret message written in the grain of the wood that could tell me what to do.

Greg put down my drawings and took a sip of coffee from a mug beside him, keeping the gun trained on me. "I made some coffee. Hope that's okay. Would you like a cup?"

I tried to pull myself together and think. I had to pretend I didn't know anything. He had to believe I thought of him only as Greg, Louisa's brother, not as Giles Leonard, the artist who had stolen his sister's art.

"I- I don't understand, Greg. What's with the gun? Is this some kind of a joke?" I said, trying to pretend. But I knew by his expression it was hopeless.

He smiled. "It's a good thing you're a picture book writer, not an actress. I don't think you would've gotten very far as an actress, Sarah."

I tried again. "What's going on, Greg?

He smiled slightly and shook his head. "Better, Sarah. But still no academy awards for you. No. I really think you should stick to picture books. That's where your talents lie. You know that."

"Please, Greg. I don't understand. Why have you broken in to my house?"

"Oh, I didn't break in. I have a key. I've had one for weeks now. You really should be more careful about where you hide them, Sarah."

I tried again. "Look, I haven't told anyone about Louisa. I won't tell anyone. You can meet with Daniel Hollister. Tell him whatever you want. Either way, you'll get the money, right?"

"Oh yes. I'll get the money. But this isn't really about the money. Not anymore. You know that, Sarah."

"No, I- I don't know what you're talking about, Greg."

He looked awful. Like he hadn't slept in days. He took out a flask and poured something that looked and smelled like bourbon into his coffee cup.

"Oh, but I think you do. I really think you do. See, I've thought for a while now that you might know, and I had to find out. It's a shame, really. I was really hoping you didn't know. You seemed like such a trusting person, Sarah."

He sighed, sipped his coffee and went on. "But when I heard you'd been to see Al Dugan, well, then I knew it was only a matter of time until you figured it out."

"Figured what out, Greg? I don't know what you're talking about. Honest."

"Don't mess with me like this, Sarah. I know you were snooping around, trying to get answers. I know all about what Sam Pryor told you." He narrowed his eyes. "Sam Pryor. That son of a bitch. If he had kept his nose where it should be, we wouldn't be here, would we, Sarah?"

"I- I don't know-"

His fist hit the table. "Don't say that again! You do know. You know exactly what I'm talking about. It was

147

Sam Pryor that kept talking to you. Persuading you that Giles Leonard was an evil s.o.b."

Greg took another gulp of his coffee and went on. "But Sam Pryor didn't know dog shit about it. He didn't know how years ago Louisa begged and begged me to help her sell her work. How she was so shy she couldn't talk to anyone, and how she would start shaking whenever she had to visit a gallery that might want to buy her work."

I looked at him. In spite of the gun still pointing my way, I was curious. Besides, I thought, they always said to get them talking, didn't they?

"So that's how it started?" I asked.

He nodded. "That's how it started. So many years ago. We were both artists, only I was blocked. She was always much more productive than I was. But she couldn't stand the selling part. Just couldn't stand it. I told her I'd make up a pseudonym. The name, Giles Leonard, would be both of us, I told her. She liked that idea. But then, gradually, I had to take on Giles's persona. I had to become Giles Leonard. Do you see? Why do you think her paintings started selling so well?"

Because they're beautiful, I thought, but I said, "Because you marketed them. You created an aura around them." Stroke his ego. Buy some time. Keep him talking.

"Exactly. And for the first five years, everything was great. I made appearances in New York. I created a buzz. I was Giles Leonard. We sold the paintings, and the price kept going up. It was exciting. And lucrative. I shared the money with her, of course. And she loved it."

He stopped, looking wistful, remembering the good old days I guessed.

"But then, Louisa, silly fool, decided she didn't like it. She accused me of keeping most of the money, but she didn't realize how much it all cost. Jesus. The expenses."

"I can imagine. It must have been terribly costly."

He nodded. "Louisa didn't understand. She hated New York. Never went there. Gradually I had to stop making appearances. It was taking its toll on my health. I was drinking more than I should have. Louisa heard some things. She threatened to stop painting."

"But you were just trying to help her," I said.

He nodded. "She never understood that." He said it so sadly. Sounded so regretful. For a second I almost felt sorry for him. Then I remembered the enormity of what he'd done, and fear swept over me like a cold wind. I sat on my hands so he wouldn't see how badly they were shaking.

"Finally," he went on, "I made up the story about Giles Leonard moving to the south of France and shipping occasional paintings back home. I moved back up to Maine. Became Greg Myner again, hoping that would make Louisa happy.

"She was living in DC at the time, painting. She didn't go out much. Didn't see many people. She came up to Maine for the summers. But she started getting more and more unstable. She slashed up that painting. Refused to paint. Then she started going to that shrink, whoever he was. Or she. Louisa would never tell me who it was. That's when things got bad. Louisa changed. She wanted to paint under her own name. But it was too late for that. She just couldn't see that.

"She moved over here. Told me she had stopped painting. I believed her at first. I still had some of her old paintings, enough to bring in a little money. But once they were gone I had nothing. I begged her to start painting again, but she said no.

"Then I found out about the studio. She never told me about it. Tried to hide it from me. But I followed her one day. I couldn't believe when I saw it. All those paintings, just sitting there. And meanwhile, neither of us had any money. Well, she had some stashed away, but I was dead broke."

"That must have been hard for you. After all you did for her," I said.

"You have no idea." Keeping the gun trained on me, he poured some more bourbon into his coffee cup. He took a long sip and then went on. "She let me take some of the paintings from the studio, and I managed to sell one or two, but she wouldn't let me take enough for a show.

"Then she did that picture book. She told me I could still sell the paintings as Giles Leonard, but she wanted to use her own name on the book. I tried to make her see that

149

that wouldn't work. You've seen it. It's obviously the same work."

I nodded. "It's very distinctive work."

He frowned and shook his head. "I did everything I could to make her understand, but she wouldn't let it go."

He sighed and took a swig right from his flask, giving up on the coffee cup. "I miss her, you know. We were so close. Twins. I told you that, didn't I? When we were kids we were always together. Louisa was so shy. She counted on me for everything. She always listened to me. And I always took care of her. I always did."

"You did the best you could, Greg," I said.

He nodded. "If it hadn't been for that damn picture book."

"*Jesse's Secret.*"

"Jesse's god damned Secret. She kept on and on about it. No one would make the connection. Which was utter bullshit. I kept telling her it wouldn't work. Publish it under Giles Leonard, or let it go."

Another swig.

"Then she just stopped talking about it. Acted like she'd forgotten all about it. But I knew that was bullshit. I knew she was up to something. I came back here, but I didn't tell her I was here. I followed her. Saw her meet with you. That night I confronted her about it. She told me about your meeting, what you had said about how great it was. And how you had given her the name of a publisher.

"She told me there was a new book too. That you had it, and that she was going to take your class. I broke into your place a few days after that, looking for the new manuscript. Well, I didn't actually break in. The place was wide open. And I figured I'd blame it on Louisa if anyone figured it out. Fortunately the cops in this shithole town are brain dead." He took another pull on the flask.

"You really should be more careful about your keys, Sarah. Hiding those keys all over," he smiled slightly and shook his head. "Not too smart."

Was he starting to slur a little? Was this good or bad? Was he more dangerous drunk? Maybe he would pass out and I could run. Whatever, I had to keep him talking.

"So you took the new manuscript?" I asked, shivering even more at the thought of this nut case sneaking around my house and office.

He nodded. "But not till later. After she was dead. When I couldn't find it the first time I went back and begged her not to publish or to publish it as Giles Leonard. I figured we could tell you she had shown it to you as a favor to him. I told her I'd expose her, and tell everyone she was crazy. She said she didn't care. No one would believe me. She could prove they were her paintings. The next day when she was at her studio I went back and took *Jesse's Secret*. I went to New York so it would be post marked from there, and sent it to that publisher under the name Giles Leonard. I figured once it was done she'd calm down about it. And god knows we needed the money. Then I went back up to Maine. She called that night when she got home and couldn't find the manuscript. I told her what I had done and she went nuts. I said I'd come back down there the next day and we'd talk it all out."

"And you did?"

He nodded. "I was sure she'd listen. She had always listened to me. The last few years she'd been harder to reason with, but in the end she had always listened." He looked at me. "Always."

"Of course. She knew you had her best interests at heart."

"But this time it was different. She was determined. And she was furious. Said she was sick of it all and she was going to go to you and tell you the whole story. She knew you'd believe her."

I stared at him, trying to imagine how Louisa must have been feeling.

"I told her to calm down, that we could talk it out. I fixed us both a drink, and slipped a few xanax into hers."

"And then she killed herself?" I asked.

He looked at me sharply, eyes narrowed, trying to gage my sincerity. "But you don't believe that, do you, Sarah? Sam Pryor made sure you wouldn't believe it."

Of course I didn't believe it. But I wasn't about to tell him that.

151

"I don't know what you mean, Greg. Look, you've been through enough. I understand that. No one can ever prove that Louisa and Giles were the same person."

He sighed. "I wish it were that simple, Sarah."

"What do you mean, Greg?"

He didn't say anything for a minute, and for that minute I allowed myself to hope that maybe he was reconsidering. Maybe he would just let me go. And I would call the police the minute he was gone.

"I like you, Sarah. I really do," he said.

"I like you too, Greg. You know that."

He shrugged. "Maybe you do. But it doesn't matter now. You know too much. I've been watching you for a while now. You and your family."

The full horror of this swept over me. I felt sick, then faint. I couldn't speak.

He sat back and looked at me. "After all, Sarah, I had to find out where the new manuscript was hidden. I got some first class binoculars and I watched you all. Sometimes from my car, sometimes from a boat, sometimes from the woods."

I thought about the figure I had seen on the shore and Paddington barking. I was shaking uncontrollably. I tried not to show it, but he could tell.

He smiled. "I got to know your routines. In the morning, light in the kitchen, light in the hall. Dog out, newspaper in. Figures moving to and fro across the window. Like watching a toy family. Or a family in a snow globe."

I felt so sick. It was all I could do not to scream, or cry, or collapse right there, but I couldn't. I couldn't. I had to hold it together. Keep him talking, I told myself.

"So Greg, how did you find the manuscript? How did you know it was at the Art Center?"

"It wasn't easy, believe me. Like I said, I watched you. And I knew it wasn't in your house. I stole your keys to the Art Center. Went in after dark. Frankly, Sarah, I'm surprised your office was locked, after how careless you are about your house."

"The doors lock automatically, Greg. I probably wouldn't lock up every night if not."

He nodded. "Figures. Then I even drove back out to your place that night and left your keys by your car."

"Yes. I remember. I thought they'd fallen out of my purse. It was a long day."

"Tell me about it."

"So you have everything, Greg. There's nothing to worry about. It's all over."

"I'd love to believe that, Sarah. But you and I both know it's not true." He frowned. Took a big swig from his flask. "It might have been all over if it wasn't for that asshole Sam Pryor."

"Sam Pryor?"

"Don't play stupid, Sarah. You think I'm a fool?"

"I don't, Greg. But Sam's dead. Maybe you didn't know."

"You're funny, Sarah. You are really funny."

"I really didn't know him well, Greg. I just heard through the grape vine that his house had burned and he'd burned with it."

"That's bull shit."

"He called me a few times asking if I knew Louisa. I said I'd met her once." I tried to give a nonchalant shrug, but I was shaking so hard it probably came off looking more like seizure. "Frankly, Greg, I know you better than I ever knew Louisa or Sam. I met her once. So I don't understand-"

"Shut up, Sarah! Just shut up! Just listen, okay?"

"Okay."

"Sam Pryor didn't know the first thing about Louisa. And he had that fucking notebook."

"But the notebook is gone, Greg. It was burned up in the fire. There's no other proof of anything. You're in the clear."

"Did you hear me? I said shut up!"

"Right. Sorry."

"The notebook wasn't burned up. I have the notebook. I told your editor- our editor- I had proof. The proof is the notebook."

I tried to smile. "Well, there you are, Greg. You've got proof. There's nothing to worry about."

He shook his head, almost sadly. "It's too late, Sarah."

"You keep saying that Greg, but-"

He hit the table again. "Because it's true. And you know it. That night, when she passed out, I put her in the dory and rowed out into the Choptank." He paused. "She didn't suffer. She never knew what happened."

"Greg, I believe you. She would have done it herself anyway. She'd already tried. I know you only did what you had to..."

"I really wish I could believe that, Sarah. But I don't."

He was slurring his words. He took another swig from his flask, and I was thinking maybe I could just keep him talking until he passed out, but...what time was it? How much time did I have till the kids came home? I couldn't have him here when they came home. I decided this had gone on long enough. I needed to get him out of the house. Time was ticking away. What if one of them came home early... I felt faint at the thought. All I wanted to do was get him out of my house, even if I had to go with him, which I knew I would.

"Look, Greg. Like I said, I'm on your side, but even if you don't believe that, what's your plan here? You can't just shoot me and leave. There will be an investigation. People will find out it was you."

"I know that, Sarah. I know that. You must think I'm pretty stupid if you think I'd do that."

"No-" I started to say, but he waved the gun, telling me to be quiet. He took another sip from his flask. I kept quiet. Very quiet. Whatever you say, Greg old boy.

He looked out the window. "It's such a pretty day, isn't it? And warm, for this time of year. Shurprisingly warm. I thought we might take a sail. Might be the last one of the season."

Or the last one period, for me at least, I knew he was thinking. But when I heard that I was happy- well, happy is not exactly the right word here, but all things are relative, right? More than anything I wanted him out of the house. I wanted him as far away from my children as I could get him, and if that meant going for a sail, well, fine by me. Besides, I knew that sailboat as well as I knew my own manuscripts. Even though he had the gun and 70 or 80 pounds on me, being on the boat would equal the playing field a bit. And I had something he didn't have:

sheer, dogged, unwavering determination that I was *not* going to die. My children had already lost one parent. They were not going to lose another.

I wasn't about to let Greg see that I liked the idea of a sail. He might change his mind, or he might be more on guard. I wanted him to let his guard down. Get a bit complacent.

"It- it's pretty cold out, Greg. Colder than you think. Especially once you're out on the water."

"Oh, but Sarah, you've forgotten. I'm from Maine. This is a beautiful fall day for us Maineiacs."

"But, I- I'm not sure the boat is seaworthy right now. I haven't been out in a few weeks. I should have put it up for the winter by now. But..."

"Not to worry, Sarah. I know you're an expert sailor. And I'm not so bad myself. We'll just go for a friendly sail and see what we come up with. How about it?"

"Whatever you say, Greg."

"And maybe we should have a picnic while we're out. Just something simple. You know, wine, cheese, bread. Do you have any French bread, Sarah?"

He took another swig of the bourbon or whatever it was from his flask.

"I might have a loaf in the freezer. Let me check." I stood up slowly. He pressed the gun into my back and we went downstairs into the kitchen. He sat at the kitchen table holding the gun on me while I went to work on our picnic. Making a picnic while there's a gun trained on you is no easy feat, let me tell you. I wondered if I should try to stuff a knife down my jeans. But what if he saw me? I was hyper aware of that gun as it moved along with me. It's amazing how difficult it is to think straight when there's a gun pointed at you.

I decided not to worry about the knife. There were knives on the boat, and anyway, wasn't it better to get him out of the house? Away, far far away from my children? I started to shake badly. Stop. I told myself. I could not think about my children. I could not go to pieces. I needed all my wits about me.

I found a loaf of bread in the freezer, and took some cheese from the fridge.

"What about wine, Sarah?" he asked.

"Wine! Of course. Wine!" I grabbed a bottle from the bar. "And do you want a refill for your flask, Greg?"

He grinned. "Sure, Sarah. Good idea." I reached for the flask, but he held up his hand. "Bring me the bottle. I'll fill it. Don't want you slippin' a little something extra in there."

Actually, it hadn't occurred to me, but now that he said it I wished it had. Except what? Would Tylenol PM do it? And wouldn't it taste funny? Oh God. He was right. I was a picture book artist, not a criminal.

But the whiskey was doing its own good work, although I prayed it would make him pass out, and not just get even crazier and more dangerous.

"We'd better get some foul weather gear, don't you think?" I said. "It'll be freezing out there."

"Yeah. Do you have something I can wear?" he asked.

"Of course," I told him. "It's all in the mudroom. We can get it on our way out."

I packed the wine and food into a cooler. "Ready?" I said brightly, as if I was trying to look forward to our little sail.

He stood up and came up behind me. He thrust the gun against my back and said, "Just walk slow, and don't try to run. I'll have to shoot you if you so much as take a step away. Understand?"

"I understand."

I picked up the cooler and tried to move slowly and steadily. In the mudroom I handed him an old barn coat of Tom's. The thing was absolutely the worst possible garment to be wearing if he should take an unplanned swim. For myself I chose one of the new survival jackets that Geordie, Mr. Worst Case Scenario, had made us get. It was super light weight, acted like a wet suit, and had built in flotation devices that activated automatically, but didn't prohibit swimming. My cell phone was still in my pocket from my walk. Once I was on the boat I would slip it into the waterproof pocket in the survival jacket.

I was worried that Greg would notice the difference in our apparel, but either he was too drunk or too stupid to notice. I also changed into lightweight, cold weather boat boots.

And then I was leading him away away away from my children, thank god, thank god, thank god. In spite of the hard cold steel barrel of his gun digging into my back, I could have wept with relief when I finally got him out of my house.

Paddington followed us, sensing something strange was up, but not knowing what to do about it. I tried to send her a telepathic message. Think, Paddy, think. If ever there was a time to put that little brain of yours in gear and pull a Lassie, this is it.

We went slowly across the lawn down to the dock. There was no one out on the water. There was no one who could have seen him and wondered what a strange man was doing on the Landings' boat.

We untied the boat and then Greg told me to get on board and start rigging her up. He stood on the dock above me, holding the line with one hand and the gun with the other. He was already swaying a bit from the alcohol. Once on board it would be worse. I began to formulate a plan.

When we were ready to go, Greg came aboard and shoved us off, and we headed up river with me at the helm and him sitting behind me, gun in one hand, whiskey flask in the other. The whiskey was definitely taking its toll. He was slurring badly and beginning to ramble. I knew I didn't have too much time. As soon as we rounded the point, the breeze picked up and I suggested he raise the sails. He did, wobbling a lot, and almost falling several times. Once the sails were up I cut the engine.

Thank god there was a nice off shore breeze, so it made sense to stay reasonably close to shore.

Greg kept sipping and seemed to forget what we were doing out here. He stretched out a bit, and actually turned his face to the sun. The breeze picked up, and I knew it was time to make my move. I pulled the face protector over my mouth and nose, spun the wheel, cut the jib and jumped.

Chapter Twenty-Two

The water was freezing. Thank god I was wearing Geordie's survival jacket. I swam towards shore as if propelled. I wasn't sure what had happened to the boat, or if he had fallen into the river. I didn't care. I just swam. I heard Greg shouting, then I heard shots, but by that time I was pretty far from the boat, and he was drunk. I submerged, hoping he would think he had got me, and continued toward shore. He fired a few more shots, and then he must have attempted to get the boat back on tack. By that time I had almost reached the shore, and though I was exhausted, I pushed on.

I swam and swam, but the shore seemed to stay the same distance away, or possibly even get farther. Was the tide against me? Was I going backwards? I tried not to think, but to save my energy. I was growing exhausted, and I knew that if I didn't get there soon I would get hypothermia and drown. I remembered when Gracie had been on the swim team years ago, when she had won a meet we had thought she never would she had said, "My arms and legs were so tried I didn't think they would keep moving, but they did!" Keep moving, arms and legs. Then Justin, "Get that runner's high. Mom, you can do it." Geordie said, "You won't freeze mom. That's a survival suit." And Tom said, "You cannot leave them alone, Sar. You can not do that." And then I felt mud beneath my fingers. I crawled up the bank and with my last few ounces of strength I pulled my cell from the watertight pouch in my suit and dialed 911. Then I stumbled through the woods and collapsed not too far from the road.

In my dream Justin and Grace were arguing. I couldn't make out the words. Then I heard Grace say, "Shhh. She's waking up. Act human for once," and I realized I wasn't dreaming.

I opened my eyes and saw three faces peering down at me. I smiled, and put one arm around Geordie, and he hugged me awkwardly and curled up next to me on the bed. Grace took my other hand and leaned down to give me a kiss. Justin moved back and began pacing behind Grace. "Jesus, Mom. You have to be the only person in the world who could make being a picture book artist into a dangerous profession!" Then they all began talking at once, until a nurse came by and took things in hand.

"Your mom needs to rest, kids," she said, shooing them away. "If we let her get her rest, she'll be good as new tomorrow."

Apparently the paramedics had found me quite soon after I had collapsed, so I would not suffer any permanent consequences of the hypothermia.

"Aren't glad you wore your survival jacket?" Geordie said.

"I sure am," I told him. It had probably saved my life.

I dosed on and off for the rest of the day and night, and the following morning my doctor pronounced me good to go. He gave me a prescription for pain, though I really wasn't in any physical pain. He also gave me a prescription for tranquilizers. I had always hated tranquilizers, but this was one time when I thought I could use them. Every time I thought of Greg Myner sneaking around our house, watching us from the woods, following us in the car I started to shake like an overloaded washing machine.

I learned they had found him on the boat, almost passed out and far out in the Bay, the boat sailing along practically by itself. I told the police everything I knew. Greg was in jail, without bail, pending a hearing, and no doubt a trial, for the murders of Louisa Myner, Sam Pryor, and the attempted murder of Sarah Landing.

Two days later I was in my office working on the sequel to *Wellington's Wand* when the doorbell rang, and Paddington went into watch dog mode. Too bad she hadn't done that when Greg Myner was holding a gun to my back. But maybe it was just as well, because I wouldn't have put it past Greg to shoot poor Paddington on the spot.

I went to the door with some trepidation. Even though I knew Greg Myner was safely put away in jail with no chance of bail, I was still very very shaky from the whole experience. I opened the door but left the chain in place and peered out to see Daniel Hollister.

"I just had to see that you were-" he began, but I cut him off.

"One sec," I said slamming the door in his face, zipping the chain off and throwing the door wide. And then, bizarrely, I was in his arms. I don't know how it happened, or which of us made the first move, I just know that it happened, and it felt so good.

He held me close for a minute. "I've been frantic," he said. Then he seemed to realize what he was doing and he pushed me away as if I had suddenly burst into flames. "I'm sorry. I'm so sorry, Sarah. But I've been frantic ever since I heard what happened. I had to come and see for myself that you were okay."

I stepped back and held the door open. "Come in," I said. He was wearing jeans and a pale blue chambray shirt under a brown suede jacket. His dark hair was longer than the last time I had seen him, and he looked as though he had forgotten to shave that morning.

"I just heard about this yesterday. I couldn't sleep at all last night. Finally I got up and drove straight down here. I left my place at five a.m. What time is it now?" he asked.

"It's a little after ten. You made good time," I said, smiling.

He looked at me closely. "You're okay? You *are* okay?"

"I'm fine. It wasn't one of my top ten most pleasant experiences, but it was certainly memorable." I steered him toward the kitchen. "Let's have some coffee."

"Coffee would be great. I've already had three Red Bulls and four cups on the drive, but that highway stuff can't really be considered coffee."

I sat him down at the table and made a fresh pot of coffee. While it was brewing I made some toast and washed some blueberries and raspberries. I put it all on the table, poured us both a cup and sat down across from him.

He stared at me, shaking his head slowly. "You're amazing. I came down here to make sure you're alright, and here you are taking care of me."

"I'm not the one who was up all night and then had a five hour drive."

He sipped his coffee. "So. Tell me everything."

"What have you heard?" I asked.

"I heard that Greg Myner broke into your house, held you up at gun point. Forced you onto the sailboat and planned to pitch you overboard, but you jumped ship and swam ashore."

I nodded. "That's pretty much what happened. Except that Greg didn't have to break in. He had a key, thanks to my brilliant policy of hiding keys in five accessible places. I took Paddington out for a walk, and when I came back he was sitting in my office with his gun and a flask full of whiskey."

"Jesus."

"Yes. It was a trifle unnerving."

"He's a nutcase."

"To put it mildly. I tried to convince him I thought he was sweet to have helped Louisa out by stealing her paintings and murdering her, but he didn't buy it. He said he couldn't trust me not to rat him out. Then he suggested I make a picnic and we go for a sail."

"A picnic?"

"With wine."

"Of course."

"I mentioned that it might be a tad chilly out on the water, this being late November, but he reminded me that he's from Maine and used to cold weather sailing."

"Jesus."

I filled Daniel in on the rest of my adventure, and he asked, "So you called the police and then passed out."

"Yes. Luckily they found me pretty soon after I passed out. "

"And Greg stayed on the sailboat?"

I nodded. "He was halfway across the bay when they picked him up. So drunk he could hardly walk. It's amazing he could sail the boat. I don't know what his plan was. Or if he even had one."

"And he confessed?"

"Apparently. I guess he broke down and told them everything. There's going to be a trial, and he's in prison without bail right now. What's going to happen to *Jesse's Secret?*"

"We'll publish it under Louisa's name. As soon as we get the go ahead from the judge in charge of things. It'll probably be held up for a while while we figure out who holds the copyright, but it will be published. And it will be published under Louisa's name."

"That's great. I just wish she could be here to see it."

"And how is your new book coming?"

"It's coming. I'm actually really excited about it."

"That's great. No repercussions from your adventure?"

"No. In fact, yesterday and today have both been great. I think I'm just glad to be alive."

"I'm glad you're alive too," he said, taking my hand. "And there's something I need to talk to you about."

He seemed nervous, and I got worried. Was he canceling my contract?"

"Shoot," I said.

"Hey. I'm not Greg Myner."

"Thank god."

"Okay. Here goes." He took a deep breath. "I...I'm afraid I may not be able to be your editor anymore."

My heart sank. This was not good news.

"Really?"

"It- it's nothing bad. Nothing that will affect your contract or anything. It's just that, well, there's this policy at Pinnacle..."

"A policy?"

"Yes. A policy...oh god. I don't know how to say this." He ran his hands through his hair several times and then said, "I think I'm falling in love with you. I know you don't even know me that well. You probably think I'm crazy. It's just that, I don't think I can be a good editor when I feel this way about you."

I stared at him, not sure what to say, not sure how I felt. "Oh," I said finally.

"Look. I don't expect you to feel the same. I know you probably don't. It's just that, I do. I can't help it. I, ethically, I can't continue as your editor."

I nodded.

"But don't worry. You're going to have Gineva Barnes. She's the best. Much better than me. Really. And she loves your work. And, and she's had much more experience with picture books than I have. Really. I promise. She'll be better for you."

"But I don't want Gineva Barnes," I said.

"Do you know her?" he asked.

"No."

"Than how do you know you don't want her?"

"Because I want you."

"But there is a policy at Pinnacle-"

"Who cares about their stupid policy?"

"Well, it's not only that. I just know I can't be objective here..."

"But you're the best editor I've ever had."

"Gineva will be better. I promise," he stood up. "I should go. I just had to make sure you were alright and..."

"Where are you going?"

"Back to New York. Back to work."

"So you can...not be my editor?"

He shrugged. "Sarah. I don't know what else to do. I can't help the way I feel."

The thought of him leaving and going out of my life was too horrible. I realized I was falling in love with him too. I just hadn't known it until that moment.

"Don't go," I said, starting to cry...

"You want me to stay?"

I nodded. I was crying and then I started making strange hiccupping noises.

"Are you okay?"

"I'm fine," I said, crying and hiccupping.

"You don't sound very fine."

I grabbed a dish towel and wiped my face. I took a deep breath. "I'm fine," I said again. I started crying again, sobbing actually.

He sat down. "It's okay. It's okay, Sarah."

"I know." I took a deep breath. Got myself sort of under control. "It's just the thought of you leaving was terrible."

"It was?"

"Yes."

"I won't leave then."

"Okay."

He got a clean dish towel and put cold water on it and tenderly wiped my face.

"I'll stay as long as you want."

"Okay."

He kissed me. "But I can't be your editor."

"Okay."

My cell phone rang. I picked it up and heard Geordie's voice. "Mom?"

"Yes, sweetie. Are you alright?"

"I'm fine. But I forgot my lunch."

"Oh. Well, I'm coming into town anyway. I'll drop it off."

"Thanks, Mom."

I hung up and looked at Daniel. "Geordie forgot his lunch. I have to drop it off."

"Can I come?"

"Hmm. I don't know. You're not my editor anymore."

"But I can still be a lunch dropper-offer."

"I suppose so."

"And I could still buy you a lunch."

"Are you sure? It's not against Pinnacle's policy?"

"Definitely not."

"I am kind of hungry."

"And I could buy you dinner later."

"Let's take it one meal at a time," I said. I took his hand. "Geordie's lunch first. Then lunch for us. And after that, who knows?"

Made in the USA
Middletown, DE
27 February 2021

34465228R00096